TRITON

A BAD BOY SEAL ROMANCE

ALANA ALBERTSON

Bolero
Books

TRITON
Copyright © 2017 by Alana Albertson
Cover design by Regina Wamba of MaeIDesign.com
Cover Photography: Eric Battershell Photography
Cover Model: Chase Bergner

Bolero Books, LLC
11956 Bernardo Plaza Dr. #510
San Diego, CA 92128
www.bolerobooks.com

🌸 Created with Vellum

I must be a mermaid . . . I have no fear of depths and a great fear of shallow living.

— ANAÏS NIN

TRITON: A BAD BOY SEAL ROMANCE

Aria—I teach mermaid fitness at a ritzy hotel next to the Naval Amphibious Base. I know better than to let one of those famous frogmen chase my tail. But in a moment of weakness, I submit to Erik, a tattooed badass Navy SEAL. After one night of incredible passion, I can't stop thinking about his cocky ways and his dirty mouth.

But I am about to train to be the first female Navy SEAL.

When I show up on the first day of training, I'm horrified to realize that Erik is my BUD/S instructor. He's the only person who stands in the way of me achieving my dream.

I'm not a quitter. He can taunt me, tease me, and run me ragged, but I'll never ring that bell.

Erik—Aria is the most incredible woman I've ever met. She won the gold medal for synchronized swimming, and she looks like a little mermaid the way she moves underwater. Once I find out that the sexy redhead is teaching aquatic classes next to my base, I vow to do anything to make her mine.

After a mind-blowing month together, she tells me she needs to go away to train. I assume it's for another synchro competition.

I'm dead wrong.

She shows up in BUD/S as a member of the first class to let in women. And I'm her instructor.

There's no way in hell I will lower the standards of my Team to please the brass and make a political statement.

It doesn't matter how much I want her because she's forbidden to me now. She will obey my every command.

She can try to pass hell week, but she will fail.

I'm a Navy SEAL, a Triton, a god of the sea.

And she will never be part of my world.

1

ERIK

In the water, out of the water. Pain for you, fun for me.

I placed my hand over the raised motto printed on the back of my long-sleeved, dark blue instructor shirt from my locker in the BUD/S compound. Warmth filled my chest as I pulled the shirt over it.

Today was going to be epic.

It was my first day as a BUD/S instructor—responsible for training the next generation of Frogmen. Only eight years ago, I'd been a mere tadpole myself. My instructors were such badasses, and now it was my turn to inflict the hurt. After surviving many deployments with SEAL Team Seven, I had been graced with this coveted non-deployable three-year land duty. Three years stateside in beautiful Coronado, California—home to the sexiest women in the world. Yup, there were plenty of fish in the sea.

Maybe I would finally get over Aria.

My buddy Devin walked into the room. With his pretty boy swagger, long blonde hair, steel-grey eyes, and movie star smile, there was no doubt that he used to be a world-famous rock star, even though he kept his true identity a fiercely guarded secret. The guys had nicknamed him, "Skin," because, like Rumpelstiltskin, he never would admit to anyone outside of the Teams that he had once graced the cover of Rolling Stone shirtless and clad in skin tight leather pants. He had abandoned his former life as Dax, lead guitarist of Gold Whiskey, the millennium's hottest heavy metal band, to become an operator.

I couldn't fathom ever earning that much money and then giving it up. And as much as I loved my job, I struggled to accept the fact that even though I risked my life daily to protect America, on my salary, I would never be able to save enough money to buy a home where I was stationed. Any extra income I made, I sent to my mom. She was proud and humble and would always refuse to accept it, only to eventually give in reluctantly. Ever since my dad had died, she had done her best to provide for my sister but struggled to make ends meet. I was determined to help them any way I could.

Devin's hand brushed his long blonde bangs off his face. "Hey, dude. Have you seen the Frog Princess?"

Fuck. Just my fucking luck. My first time as an instructor and I had to be responsible for the downfall of the Teams. Today was the day that Naval Special Warfare would lose all its standards. Despite the Team guys' collective protests and pleas, our arguments had failed to convince the high brass of the Navy, who quite frankly didn't know shit, that having a female on the Teams was the worst idea imaginable. Fuck political correctness—I was training warriors.

I exhaled. "Nah, man. I just hope she looks like Demi Moore. Maybe we should assemble a special Team, just of women. Wait until their times of the month sync up, then deploy them. They will lay waste to the enemy."

Devin burst into laughter. "Damn straight. They could take out ISIS."

Ha! "Fuck yeah." I fastened my boots, pushed back my sunglasses, and walked around the corner, preparing to meet my class. I gazed out at the midnight blue ocean, barely visible at zero dark thirty. The waves rippled in the distance, and the scent of salt water and sweat lingered in the air. These recruits didn't have a clue what they were about to endure.

Let the games begin.

As I approached the class, my eyes were immediately drawn to the lone female in the group, as if her presence was a magnet to my cock. The tight, brown shirt clung to her breasts, and the green cammies hung low on her slender hips. Like a flame, one wisp of her red hair peeked out of her cap. She must've felt my gaze because she raised her eyes to meet mine.

Holy fuck!

My heart pounded in my chest, and my body shook with fury.

No, she didn't look like Demi Moore. She was hotter, way fucking hotter. She wasn't anything like the type of woman I had thought would've signed up for this torture. She wasn't hardened, mean, nor did she have a chip on her shoulder.

I knew this because I knew her.

I'd loved her.

And she'd left me.

Aria stood in front of me—my little mermaid who had swum off in the middle of the night, leaving me heartbroken. She'd told me she had gone to "train." My dumb ass thought she'd meant for another shot at the Olympics. But she'd taken on the ultimate challenge.

She was here to be the first female Navy SEAL.

And I was her instructor.

I narrowed my gaze on her, purposefully intimidating her. Her chin dropped, and her eyes blinked rapidly.

My annoyance flared. What the fuck was she doing here? When had she been commissioned by the Navy? Was this why she had left me?

A tremble took over her body.

It could've been from the chill of the early morning.

Or it could've been from the horror of realizing she had come face to face with the man she had betrayed.

A man who was now in control of every second of her life. A man who now would stand in the way of her achieving her dreams.

She had lied to me about her future plans. Used me to gain access to the SEAL "O" course. Pumped me for information about BUD/S training. But even worse, she had grown close to my family. All the while knowing that she had planned to betray me.

Now I would make her pay.

I grabbed the microphone, forcing myself to calm my voice, and looked directly at her. "Welcome to BUD/S Class 334. I'm Instructor Anderson. Many have tried, few have succeeded. Drop to the ground and give me a hundred pushups."

Before I could blink her firm, tight body was parallel to the floor as she knocked out her exercise with perfect form.

I yelled into the microphone, screaming at all of my candidates. But my mind was on only one of them.

Aria.

Her sweet loving boyfriend no longer existed. It was time to introduce her to the badass Navy SEAL she had pissed off.

The warrior. The savage. The killer.

I stood behind her, my eyes focused on her firm ass.

"Eight. Nine. Ten. You think you can do this, Clements? That you are as strong as these men? You aren't. I'll tell you what you are. You're sad. You're weak. You're pathetic. This is Navy SEAL training, not water ballet. You screw up, and I'll catch you every time. I'll make you pay, princess. I'll make you pay."

"Yes, Instructor Anderson."

I got in her face. "Don't you speak. I didn't give you permission to speak. Keep that mouth of yours shut unless I tell you to open it." *To suck my cock.*

Dammit. My mind flashed to her on her knees taking me deep. Well, one of the SEAL mottos was, "Welcome the SUCK with a big hug and a smile on your face."

Fuck. I had to stop thinking about her like that.

It didn't matter how much I had once wanted her because she was forbidden to me now. I was her instructor, and she was my student.

From now on, she would obey my every command.

From now on, I was her master.

I stepped away, and she took a quick rest on her forearms. I turned right back toward her. "When I walk away, I'll still be watching you. I have eyes on the back of my head. If I tell you to do something, you do it right. If I tell you to do pushups, you do them right. Got it, cupcake?"

She grunted, and I walked away from her, trying to focus on any of the other men, any of the candidates but her.

How had I been so wrong about her? No wonder she had become so angry when I had told her I didn't think women should be SEALs. It had once even crossed my mind that there was a possibility that she wanted to be a SEAL. But I had dismissed that thought.

I'd be the laughing stock of my Team now. Devin and Kyle both knew that I had dated her. I had to steer clear of her on our off times. Any contact with her could be misconstrued as fraternization. She had wasted enough of my life —I refused to allow her to ruin my career.

Devin yelled for them to lay on their backs and start leg lovers. I grabbed my hose and blasted a stream of water into her mouth, as her legs scissored up and down. As I counted at her, I imagined that stream of water being my cum shot into her greedy little mouth.

I dropped the hose, unable to look at the wet T-shirt clinging to her chest, her nipples poking through the damp fabric.

But on a glance back, I noticed something else. Her legs were straight, and her abs were engaged. My eyes surveyed the men on the ground. Many of them were flailing around like a fish out of water, with no form at all.

Fuck my life. She was one of the best ones in the class.

But it didn't matter. I would make her ring that bell. Her betrayal of me alone should be enough to get her kicked out.

Aria and the men completed their evolution, and I yelled at them again. "This entire evolution has been pathetic. Nothing any one of you has done has been even remotely acceptable. Maybe that's because there's a woman in your class that you have all decided to lower your standards to her level."

Her eyes tore into me, and her mouth quivered. I had to look away. I couldn't deal with her emotions.

Or mine.

But I also couldn't have anyone think that I was being extra hard on her because I'd fucked her. It wasn't just her future on the line—it was mine too.

I threw her a bone.

"But, you are all wrong. We will never lower our standards. Not for the Frog Princess or for any of you fools. And I'll tell you what. The Frog Princess showed you all up tonight. If you can't do as many leg lovers as a girl, none of the rest of you have the right to be here. 'Lady' and Gentlemen, it's going to be a long, cold, wet night."

I threw down my microphone and walked away. Inwardly, I winced— she'd made a fool out of me.

But I knew how to make her crack. How to make her doubt herself.

I knew her Achilles heel.

She would never pass the "O" course because she would never master the Dirty Name obstacle.

When I heard that sweet chime of the bell that she would ring, I would breathe a sigh of relief. For that sound would mean that I'd never have to see her again.

The sooner, the better.

She could try to pass BUD/S, but she would fail.

I was a Navy SEAL, a Triton, a god of the sea.

And she would never be part of my world.

2

ARIA

SEVEN MONTHS EARLIER

"**B**ye Flounder. Mommy will be home in a few hours." I rubbed my beagle's ears, threw him a toy, and locked my rented beach cottage.

Flounder was my right-hand companion. He was now in his twilight years, and my heart ached thinking about the day when I would have to endure my life without him. That dog had been through everything with me. Homeschooling, attending Stanford, training for the Olympics, and ultimately winning the gold in synchronized swimming. When I'd discovered him at a shelter with an ear tumor, a skin infection, and droopy eyes, I knew I had to rescue him. I'd named him Flounder as a joke. After all, my nickname was America's Little Mermaid.

Sure, the redheaded synchronized swimming champion

named Aria would draw comparisons to the beloved fable. But my journey had been more than a coincidence. It was almost as if my fairy tale had been predestined. My teenaged mother had been a synchro competitor but had to quit training when she had become pregnant with me. The second she found out that I was a girl, she had planned my entire life. I started swim lessons when I was an infant, began synchro classes with the world-renowned Marin Mermaids when I was four, was recruited to compete for Stanford at eighteen, and was selected for the Olympic team when I turned twenty-one.

After I had won the gold last summer, reporters constantly asked me if I planned to take a break. Travel. Relax. Go on *Dancing under the Stars*. Experience life, fall in love.

But I didn't know the meaning of the word break.

I was only twenty-three. I wasn't done achieving my goals.

In fact, I had just joined the Navy.

I had considered many positions in the military. A linguist, due to my love of foreign tongues and travel, an intel officer, due to my desire to discover secrets, and a diver, due to my love of the water. But ultimately, I kept focusing on one job.

A United States Navy SEAL—the first female in Naval

Special Warfare. Why? All the usual reasons. Serve my country, save lives, free hostages, defend freedom. Competing around the world as an American had filled me with such pride. Standing at the podium hearing the national anthem when I was awarded a gold medal was one of the few times in my life that I had been brought to tears. I knew that none of my accomplishments would've been possible if I had been born in a totalitarian regime. At that moment, I vowed to give back to the country which had given me so much.

But the true reason for my desire to fight terrorists went deeper. So deep, I dared not utter it to a soul. Not to my own mother, not to my friends. Only Flounder knew my truth, and luckily for me, he would remain silent.

I just knew I could pass BUD/S. I would have no problem during Second Phase diving instruction since I was an excellent swimmer and could hold my breath. And I was physically fit and had spent my entire life training for competitions.

But another element drove me. So many people thought it was impossible for a woman to pass BUD/S.

I was determined to prove them wrong.

My own mother scoffed at me when I suggested it. "Who would marry you?" she asked. As if marrying a man should be a career goal. Her statement was even more irksome because she had cut my father out of my life, and had chosen to be a single mom. While I resented her for alienating my father, I did appreciate all the sacrifices she had made for me. But for the life of me, I couldn't understand why she would then turn around and think that I should give up a goal of mine for a man I hadn't even met. Marriage was the furthest possible thing from my mind.

But my mom wouldn't let up with her nagging. "No real man wants to date a female warrior."

That may be true, but I didn't care. Her statement was even more infuriating since she had always been so independent and was constantly saying that she didn't need a man. Either way, it didn't matter. I didn't need to earn the title of Mrs.

The only title I cared about was Naval Special Warfare Officer.

Today I was taking my first step toward that journey.

I walked along the shore of the stunning Coronado beach. After residing in woodsy Northern California my entire life, I was thrilled to be living so close to the ocean. My rental was only for a month, but with any luck, I'd be moving here after boot camp. And with hard work, I'd be stationed here, or in Virginia Beach, for the foreseeable future.

I located the office at the Hotel Del Coronado and checked in. A stunningly gorgeous girl with long black hair framing her heart-shaped face greeted me.

"Aria? I'm Isa. I'm happy to meet you. Oh my god . . . you're so talented! I saw you win the Olympics and was blown away by your routine. I'm beyond thrilled to have you as the celebrity mermaid fitness instructor!"

Isa handed me my bright green sparkly tail and a purple bikini top. Yup, the hotel was milking *The Little Mermaid* connection for all it was worth. My hand stroked the scaly and shiny material. It would take a while to get used to swimming with my legs bound in a tail, especially since I was known for my leg work.

"Thank you. Nice to meet you too, Isa. I'm happy to be here. Are you a synchro swimmer also?"

Isa shook her head. "No, I'm a former professional ballroom dancer. Normally, I teach barre and Pilates. But I'm a decent swimmer, so I thought teaching mermaid fitness would be a great way to switch up my routine, though my husband isn't very happy with me working so close to the SEAL base. He's a Marine . . . he's not a fan of SEALs."

Husband? She looked to be around my age. I couldn't even fathom being married.

I smiled. "Oh really? Why?"

"Hubby's a war hero—jumped on a grenade. He hates to talk about his deployments—was asked to write a book but declined." Isa bit her lip. "He's very private and just doesn't like that some SEALs brag about their missions."

I tilted my head to the side. I'd met plenty of disabled vets at the Paralympics. I'd always found their stories so inspiring, and their successes seemed to evoke more emotion in them than I had seen in the competitors in my own events. "I'd love to meet him. He sounds like a great guy."

"He is. I'm lucky." Her face glowed when she talked about him—clearly, she was head over heels in love with the guy. I'd never been in love or even had a serious boyfriend. No time for romance since I had devoted my life to my sport. My personal life had consisted of drunken celebratory hookups after competitions. "Hey, we're having a party next week if you want to come."

I pursed my lips. I wasn't much of a party girl—I always felt so awkward with groups of people I didn't know. But Isa seemed so nice, so I was willing to try to attempt to come out of my shell. "I'd love that. You're the only person I know in San Diego."

"Oh. Well, I'm happy to show you around. Let start by giving you a tour of the resort."

The sight of the beautiful hotel wowed me. Like me, the Del was a redhead, and she was known as The Grand Lady of the Sea. Her glorious Victorian architecture was world famous. The crimson steeply pitched roof contrasted with the white wooden shingles. Set on the backdrop of one of the best beaches in the world, the Del was simply breathtaking.

Isa led me down the steps to the pool which overlooked the beach bordering the Naval Special Warfare base. My eyes scanned the miles of sand, towering palm trees, brick beach paths, and the ocean break, hoping to glimpse some BUD/S recruits training, but I was out of luck. I made a silent wish to see some SEALs today. I figured if I spent some time studying their training regiment, it would give me an advantage. Instead, my view consisted of classy tourists with wide brimmed hats, dark sunglasses, and couture swimwear. I definitely didn't fit in here.

Isa caught my gaze, forcing me to focus. "So, mermaid fitness is taught every Friday and Saturday at eight a.m., but the guests arrive at seven thirty. Basically, it's water aerobics and Pilates with tails and pool noodles. I used to teach Aqua Zumba, so it's a bit like that, but we can't use our legs obviously. Have you swum with a tail before?"

"I did an exhibition years ago with a tail, and sometimes my coach would bind my legs to focus on my arm movements."

"Awesome. Let's hop in, and I'll go through the routine." Isa flashed a smile and then changed out of her sweat clothes into a cute bikini, revealing her enviable swimsuit body— tan skin, huge breasts, wide hips, round booty, and a flat tummy. Sure, I was in shape, but my physique was more athletic and less bombshell. I was as pale as the San Francisco fog, had a flat chest, narrow hips, a muscular bottom, and a six-pack. As much as I had always tried to view my body as a tool to my craft and not as eye-candy, I couldn't help but be jealous of her curves. I'd love to say that I didn't care if men found me attractive or not, but that would be a lie. After years of being teased as the freckled-faced sporty redhead, I'd taken myself out of the dating game to focus on my career.

I slipped off my own pants, kept my solid black one-piece swimsuit on, stepped into the tail and pulled it up over my waist. Then I dove deep into the pool. The tight fabric constricted my legs which felt odd, but I knew I'd adjust. I could hold my breath for up to three minutes, so I glided around underwater, doing butterfly kicks. Then I hoisted my torso above the water and did a bit of my Olympic routine, not to show off, but just because I missed performing.

When I finished, Isa was clapping. "Wow, you are amazing! I could watch you all day. Maybe you could do a show at the end of class for our guests?"

"I'd love that." This would be the first summer of my life

that I wouldn't be training in the pool eight hours a day. The water was my home and being paid to be a mermaid was the perfect summer job.

"Ok. We check in the guests at quarter 'til eight. Then we issue them each a tail, a pool noodle and a towel. Once the guests put on their tails, they swim around the pool. This is much harder than it seems and the fins make big splashes, so everyone gets drenched." She splashed her own tail, creating a huge wave.

I splashed her back. "I can't wait. It sounds so much fun."

"It is. Everyone loves it. We then stand in a line and do arm exercises before we get everyone out of the pool to do ab work. We keep the music blasting to distract the students from the hard work they are doing."

I laughed. "Good strategy."

She smiled. "Then we have free swim. Of course, most of the guests use this time to take selfies or post Instagram videos. I'm sure they will want to pose with you, too. So that's about it. Do you have any questions?"

Yes. Do you know what time the SEALs train on the beach? "No. But I'm sure some will come up tomorrow."

"Cool." She squinted at the sun. "Just let me know. You will be great. Can you show me some synchro moves?"

"Sure."

We took off our tails, and I showed her some underwater split techniques. When we came up for air, I saw two bearded, ripped men in the distance run toward us dressed in cammies and tight shirts. But they weren't just any men. . . I could tell a mile away they were SEALs, storming up the beach. *My wish had come true!*

Isa rolled her eyes. "Ignore them. They run by here every day since they train just down the beach. Occasionally they will come over at the end of class and make the guests swoon."

Swooning activated. My mouth became dry. I was minutes from seeing my first SEAL in the flesh, but I wasn't another frog hog. I wanted to be just like them.

A drop dead gorgeous man with jet black hair which skimmed his forehead, electric blue eyes, and arms decorated with tattoos beelined straight towards us. His equally hot blond-haired buddy with a cocky grin stood beside him. The blonde looked familiar, but I couldn't place where I'd seen him.

I melted into the water.

"Hey, Isa. Who's your new friend?" Sexy dark-haired SEAL yelled out as he knelt next to the pool. His voice was deep and low and virile.

"This is our newest instructor. Aria—"

But before Isa could introduce me, the SEAL interrupted her, his eyes widening. "Clements. You're Aria Clements—America's Little Mermaid. The Olympic gold medalist. I'd recognize you anywhere."

He knew who I was? Most people didn't recognize me, but between my red hair and the glimpse of the routine he probably saw, I could get how someone could put it together. "Yup. That's me. What's your name?"

"Erik."

Erik? Did he say his name was Erik? Like *The Little Mermaid's* prince? I couldn't help but smile at the coincidence.

Or maybe he was messing with me.

"Nice to meet you, Erik."

"You're incredible. My little sister is a huge fan." Even though a stunningly beautiful Isa was right beside me, Erik's eyes were locked completely on mine. "I am too, by the way. So, do you live here?"

"No, just teaching here at the resort for a month." Because I'd joined the Navy and was heading to Officer Candidate School in Rhode Island and then back here on a BUD/S contract. But I kept my plans to myself. The last person I wanted to confess my desire to become a SEAL to was an active duty Frogman. From everything I'd read, the Team guys were violently opposed to integrating the Teams.

They could choke on their opinions. The defense secretary said that the Pentagon would open all combat jobs to women. Including SEALs. So these men didn't have a choice.

"Cool. Hey, I'm at work, but when I get off let me take you to dinner."

Wait *what?* Forward much? I'd never, and I meant never, been asked out on a date like that. Sure, I'd had a few internet proposals. But this guy had just met me.

My face must've shown my shock.

"I get off at six. I'll pick you up where you are staying, or we can meet here. There's this great place down the street."

Isa let out a laugh as she nudged me.

I was speechless. Did this guy want me or was he just interested in meeting an Olympian? He probably would've acted the same if he met any champion, male or female. I mean he was a SEAL. One of their mottos was "it pays to be a winner."

I wanted to *be* a SEAL, not be fucked by one. Well, that

could be fun too. But that wasn't the point. My eyes raked him up and down, drinking in his big, muscular physique. Nope . . . *not happening*. There was no way I could go out with this super-hot man and risk being distracted from my dream. I vowed to watch these SEALs from afar for a month, go to Officer Candidate School, and then finish BUD/S. There was no room for romance in my world.

"I'm not interested," I said as convincingly as I could.

Erik's mouth curved into an amused grin. "I'm not going to give up that easily, sweetheart. I always go after what I want."

Great, I had just challenged a SEAL, a man who would never quit.

"Well, good luck with that. As I said, I'm only in town for a month, so there's no point to start something we can't finish."

His eyes twinkled, and he licked his lips. Man, he was gorgeous. Maybe I had made a mistake. This could be a win-win. A hot summer romance with a sexy SEAL *and* I could glean some intel on the Teams. What could go wrong?

"Who said I wouldn't finish? I'm known to finish strong. I'll stop by tomorrow. Nice to meet you, Aria."

And with that, sexy SEAL turned and ran down the beach. His friend slapped him on the back and seemed to be joking with him.

"Oh my god . . . how cocky was that guy?" I muttered, turning my attention back to Isa. "Do you even know that dude?"

"Yeah, he comes around all the time. He's gorgeous, don't you think?"

"Uh yeah, girl. He's probably the hottest man I've ever seen."

She laughed. "Welcome to San Diego. Anyway, Erik seems nicer than the rest of them. You should just go have fun."

Fun. I didn't know the meaning of the word fun. My entire life consisted of setting goals and working hard to achieve them. But maybe Isa was right, and I should learn how to let my hair down.

We climbed out of the pool and headed toward the locker room to shower. Afterward, Isa and I exchanged numbers, we parted ways, and I walked back home. I hadn't even taught my first class, and I had already begun to lose focus. Erik was ridiculously sexy, but it didn't matter. It would be unethical to use him to gain an advantage in training, though I needed any help I could get. Honestly, winning a gold medal seemed almost easy compared to becoming the first woman to graduate from BUD/S. But I refused to let anything—or anyone—distract me.

Even if that distraction was an over six foot, fine as hell Navy SEAL.

3

ERIK

I raced down the beach, glancing back and taking another look at Aria. She had emerged from the pool, and her wet swimsuit clung to her body, showing off her incredible ass. In the water, I had seen the outline of her hard nipples. I couldn't believe that was really her. An Olympic gold medalist in my sights. Not only was she beautiful, but she was also smart and dedicated.

And flexible as fuck. I remember watching her gold medal winning routine on television last summer with my sister. At first, I thought the entire sport was creepy—the women were done up with a ton of makeup and had way too shiny hair. But once the routine started, I was blown away. Her breath control was incredible, as they were underwater for most the routine. I remembered her perfect straddle split and another part where her leg went behind her ear. I wanted to spread her legs wide on my couch and bury myself in her pussy, eating her until she came all over my face.

I couldn't wait to fuck her.

Devin hit me on the back. "Man, did you see the way that redhead opened her legs?"

Great men thought alike. "No shit, dumbass. She's Aria Clements."

Devin's gaze clouded, his expression was distant. I never knew if he was just playing with me or if he was having a flashback to his glory days.

"Who?"

"The Olympic synchronized swimming gold medalist. America's Little Mermaid. She's on a Wheaties box."

He licked his lips. "I'd love to eat her box."

I punched his arm. "Fuck off, dude. I saw her first. Did you even watch the Olympics last summer?"

"Not synchro. A bit of the swimming."

We ran back toward base. As we left the resort part of the beach and entered the restricted area, I was grateful that my place of work had multi-million-dollar views. BUD/S candidates lined the beach holding swift boats above their heads. Next year, I'd be one of the instructors. I couldn't wait to torture the next generation of SEALs.

"Well, I did. My sister is a huge fan. Aria is sexy as fuck."

Devin smirked. Nothing had changed from his rock star days—he was still a player. A different woman every night. Just as many chicks would drop to their knees to suck off a SEAL as they would to blow a rock star.

But I wasn't like him. I was picky. I wanted a woman who I could admire and respect. A woman who had goals and a life of her own. A champion, an overachiever.

Someone like Aria.

She intrigued me and was hot. Hell, she'd be a perfect partner for me in TritonFix, my side hustle.

On my rare weekends off, I provided consulting to local entrepreneurs—teaching them effective project management skills and how to work with their employees by conducting team building activities. To some of my Teammates, it sounded boring, but honestly, I loved helping the civilian world apply military discipline to business practices. And I hoped that one day it would grow into a company that could support my family.

Aria and I would make the perfect team—a SEAL and an Olympian. Clients would be knocking down my door to work with us.

In a few weeks, I was pitching a huge client. If I could promise him a session with Aria and me, I'd definitely close the deal.

But first, I had to get her to go out with me.

Devin and I hit the locker room and showered after our run. Today we had an intelligence briefing. And we'd soon deploy on an operation.

But it would be my last mission for a while.

No, I wasn't leaving the Teams. Not until I retired or died. But after eight years of training, deploying, fighting overseas, I had one more mission, and then I'd be assigned three years of shore duty. Maybe I'd be around long enough to finally have a real relationship.

I grabbed my phone and logged into the Del's website. Mermaid fitness. Tomorrow at eight a.m.

Perfect.

Grinning, I picked up the phone to call my mom.

She answered on the first ring. "Erik? What's going on, honey? Are you leaving again?"

My poor mom. Clearly, I didn't call her enough. Every time she answered the phone, she assumed that I was going to tell her I was about to deploy.

"No, Mom. I'll be around for a bit. Was just wondering if Holly would join me in Coronado for a class tomorrow."

"Of course. She'd love to go anywhere with you. What kind of class?"

"Mermaid fitness at the Del. Olympic Gold Medalist Aria Clements is teaching it."

My mom gasped. "Oh Erik, she'll be thrilled! Wow . . . Aria Clements. I love her. Do you mind if I tag along?"

Damn it. I was trying to hit on Aria. The last thing I needed was my mom cock blocking me. But I couldn't say no to her. "No, of course not. Meet me at the Del at 7:30. Traffic's pretty bad on the bridge at that time so be sure to leave early."

"I will. She'll be so excited. See you tomorrow. Love you."

"Love you, Ma. Bye."

Ah, fuck. That didn't go as planned at all. But it was my own damn fault for using my sister to get a date.

I googled Aria and watched her Olympic medal winning performance. My cock hardened as my mind flashed to the millions of positions I could fuck her in. She was so graceful, so precise. She made the moves underwater seem so effortless.

But I knew from personal experience in combat dive training that learning to hold one's breath under the water for that length of time was no easy task.

Hell, plenty of men in my own BUD/S class flunked out during dive training.

I bet Aria would pass Second Phase with flying colors.

Ha. That would be the day. There had been rumors for years now that the first female would trickle down the pipeline. A few women even passed Ranger course.

But I'd passed Ranger course, too. It was challenging, no doubt, but nowhere near as intense as BUD/S.

And the Teams weren't ready for the first female SEAL. I was so sick of arguing about it with my feminist mother. Yes, women were completely capable of achieving whatever they wanted to achieve.

But that didn't give them the right to serve in combat.

There was no place for a woman on a Team. I thought about my last deployment and couldn't imagine hiding out in the middle of the desert with a woman upsetting the balance of my men. Our Team bonded together about how much we missed pussy, liquor, and the comforts of home. We didn't need a distraction on our top-secret missions.

But I didn't need to stress about that now. I had only one thing on my mind.

Getting a date with Aria.

4

ARIA

I woke up at six a.m. after a restful night in my beach cottage. I loved this place and hoped to buy one just like it if I was stationed here. I hopped out of bed to let Flounder out and made myself a quick cup of coffee. Sitting on the porch, I appreciated the cool, ocean breeze blowing on my face. Flounder sniffed around the fragrant yellow rose bushes, and I imagined how amazing it would be to live here. Maybe after I became settled as a SEAL, I could make some time for hobbies. Take up gardening, enjoy reading a book on the beach, finally get over my irrational fear and learn how to ride a bicycle.

Maybe even find a boyfriend.

My mind immediately returned to Erik. What had he meant by saying that he would stop by tomorrow? I was nervous enough about my first-day teaching. Performing had always been easy, but interacting with the public always filled me with anxiety.

I slathered my body with sunscreen and then put the purple bikini on and then pulled up my sweats. My hair was a mess, so I secured it into a braid and made my way to the Del.

As I strolled along Ocean Boulevard a group of BUD/S candidates ran by in a pack, like hungry wolves. Their instructors drove in a truck behind them, blasting Mariachi music and yelling at them on a megaphone. I gasped, maybe this whole idea was insane. These men, all of them, were massive. Tough, strong, muscular, in perfect shape. Could I possibly compete with them? Or would I just be making a fool out of myself?

As much as I yearned to be the first female SEAL, trying and failing with the whole world watching would be humiliating. And believe me, I knew what it was like to fail, and fail big, when everyone was relying on you.

But back then, I wasn't famous.

Now, everyone had expectations of me.

I had redeemed myself with gold; most people didn't bring up the time I'd let my team down. Most people except my mother.

I went straight to the pool and found Isa waiting for me

with a big smile on her face and a wide-brimmed hat shielding her from the sun. The lush landscaping of the Del contrasted with the cloth bungalows adorning the side of the pool. With the view of the sparkling blue ocean in the background, I knew I was in paradise.

Isa removed her hat. "Hey! The guests are going to arrive any minute." She handed me a clipboard and then pointed at a bunch of papers on a kiosk. "Could you check them in while I set up the tails and pool noodles?"

"Sure."

She walked over to the side of the pool.

I scanned the list of students. But my heart stopped when I saw the final name on the list.

Erik Anderson.

Oh my god! Was Erik on the list the same person as Erik the SEAL I'd met yesterday? Is that what he meant by *I'll stop by tomorrow*?

I hurried to Isa's side. "We have a problem. Are men allowed in this class?"

Her face twisted. "Hmm. Well, they aren't banned. We haven't had any guys show up before. Is there a guy on the list?"

"Yeah. You didn't see? Erik. Isn't that the name of the SEAL we met yesterday?"

"Sure is. And I think his last name is Anderson—that's the name tape on his cammies. Damn, he must really be into you."

Dying. I was dying. I took a deep breath. "We're not actually going to let him take this class, are we?"

"I mean we can't discriminate against men. It'll be fine. He's a SEAL. I bet he will look fabulous in a tail."

I bet. I bit my lip. It was my first day, and I didn't want to argue. Especially because my whole philosophy on life was that a woman could do anything a man could do. Why shouldn't it be true in reverse?

I stood by the pool gate as the guests arrived. A few teen girls, a mother and daughter, and a couple of college-age women. And then, my heart skipped a beat.

Walking toward the pool was Erik, alongside a teenage girl who resembled him, and an older woman.

His dark hair shone in the morning sun, and his strong jaw framed his handsome face. He wore board shorts which showed off his muscular thighs and his incredible ass. How was I going to teach a class with this man in my pool?

Erik's mouth spread into a devilish grin. "Nice to see you

again, Aria." He leaned into me and gave me a hug. "I told you I'm not giving up that easily, sweetheart," he whispered in my ear.

My heart palpitated. Did this man really want to go out with me this desperately? He was fine as hell—surely he could get any woman he wanted. Feminine brunette beauties like Isa. Or blonde bombshells like some of the ladies in the pool, who were clearly checking him out, not that I could blame them. Why would he want someone as awkward as me?

But I had told him no. Something he probably wasn't used to hearing.

I inhaled him like a drug, getting high on his testosterone. He smelled minty, like a cool mojito on the rocks. I wanted to drink him up and suck him down.

I finally forced myself to peel my body off his chest. "Good to see you, too."

God, did I just say that? I am such a dork. I can't even flirt.

He winked at me. "I'd like you to meet my kid sister, Holly, and my mom, Emily."

The girl with long dark hair the shade of Erik's reached out her arms to me. "Oh my god! Aria Clements! I'm your biggest fan. I mean it. I do synchro too! My dream is to attend Stanford. You are my idol!"

I reciprocated her hug. "You are so sweet."

Their mom also hugged me. Erik had her eyes and smile. "Nice to meet you, Aria. We're honored to take your class."

"Thank you for coming today."

Holly and Emily walked over to Isa, and she handed them their tails. Erik turned around and dropped their bags near a reclining chair, lowered his large, muscular frame down into it, and relaxed back, with his hands behind his head, like he was about to watch a movie.

Oh hell no. I refused to put on a show for him.

I went over to the stash of tails and grabbed the largest bright pink one I could find and strode over to Erik.

"Class starts in five minutes." I threw it at him, and he caught it with one hand.

He pulled his sunglasses down and smirked at me. "Babe, mermaid fitness is for ladies. In case you can't tell, I'm a man."

Maybe I should tell him to prove it to me?

I could tell he was a man by that huge bulge in his board shorts. "This isn't a women's Olympic event—the class is open to both genders."

He pushed his sunglasses back on his head. "I'll just watch.

I only signed up so you wouldn't be able to kick me out of the pool area."

I laughed. "You signed up for the class, not to check out a bunch of women in bikinis. Put on your tail and dive into that pool, or I'll call security. You aren't staying at the Del. The pool is for hotel guests and participants in the class. It's your choice."

He raised his brows toward me and stood up. Before I could blink, he had ripped off his white T-shirt. Despite an effort to control myself, my jaw literally dropped, and heat spiraled through my body. Holy hell, he was fine. Abs, abs, there were abs everywhere—I counted at least eight. His perfectly crafted broad shoulders melted into incredible biceps, and he had a beautiful V-shape indentation down to his crotch revealing his sexy happy trail.

He tossed me a towel. "I'm naked under these shorts. Hold this around me so I can put on the tail."

I let out a self-deprecating laugh. Naked? The thought of him in his birthday suit accelerated my pulse. Despite my fake confidence ordering him around, his powerful presence turned my insides to mush. I wrapped my arms around his waist, holding up the towel, willing my eyes not to look at his crotch. He dropped his board shorts, and I couldn't help myself. I stole a glance, his huge cock staring back at me as he pulled up the tail.

I felt like such a pervert. His eyes gleamed when he caught the destination of my gaze, but thankfully he didn't call me out.

When he had dressed, he took the towel from my hands. "Thanks for the help. Let's do this."

And with that, Erik waddled over to the side of the pool and gracefully dived into to the deep end.

The ladies, who had now gathered in the pool, applauded and catcalled Erik like they had just been privy to a secret showing of *Magic Mike Live*.

I joined the class wading in the pool, and Isa swam up to me. "Damn, girl. He makes a beautiful Merman."

I shook my head. "Don't remind me. He's so hot . . . I don't think I can resist him."

"Then don't! He seems sweet, I mean he brought his mom and his sister. Who does that? Go out with him. Have fun. I met my hubby at a frat party. You never know how this could turn out."

I pursed my lips and nodded. I admired Isa. She seemed so fun loving and happy. No one would ever describe me as fun loving. Driven, yes, but serious. Focused. Some synchro psychopath. Over the years, I'd seen so many therapists, trying to understand my madness. The best explanation they could give me was that the absence of my father coupled with the cold parenting style of my narcissistic mother had turned me into a perfectionist. This was a bad thing that led to my bouts of depression. I always felt like people only loved me for what I achieved, not who I was.

Whatever the cause, no matter how much I fought it, I had one desire. To be the best and avoid failure at all costs. But sometimes I wished I could take a magic pill and get out of my head. Enjoy life, fall in love, relax and focus on being happy in the present instead of existing solely for the promise of a fulfilling future.

But my future could involve a hot one-night stand with this SEAL, so I was going to force myself to roll with it.

Isa grabbed the microphone. "Welcome Mermaids and Merman."

Erik waved, and my core ached. God, the things I wanted this man to do to me caused a shiver to course through my body.

"I'm thrilled to introduce you all today to our special celebrity mermaid, Olympic Gold Medalist Aria Clements!"

The ladies applauded, and Erik let out a whistle. I wanted to drown from embarrassment.

Isa continued. "We're going to have so much fun today. This is a great workout, and you get to live out your fantasy of being a mermaid. So everyone get in the pool and do a couple of laps so you can get used to your tail. Take your pool noodle and place it under your arms to stay afloat."

We dove in. Most of the ladies did some version of a leisurely breast stroke without the legs but not Erik. He didn't bother with the noodle and darted off like a missile. With a single push, he glided across the pool. The competitor in me darted to his side, determined to beat him. I charged ahead, kicking my legs in a butterfly motion and met him at the edge. Before he could touch the side of the pool, I gracefully did a somersault and sped down the other side, leaving him in my wave.

Clearly unable to back down, Erik caught up, his big, powerful arms slamming into the water, splashing me.

My heart stuttered in my chest as our eyes met and held. The moment was so hot, so electrifying, so *intimate*.

But our moment was interrupted by a bright flash. A staff photographer had taken a picture of us.

I turned my attention back to Erik. Water glistened on his tan chest. He was hot and wet and wearing nothing but a tight tail. I wanted him to pin me against the side of the pool and nail my fins to the wall. *Have mercy*.

Instead, I gave him a high five. "Good job, merman."

He smirked. "Babe, I prefer the term Triton."

Of course. Triton. A Navy SEAL. The trident was their insignia.

I met Isa back in the center of the pool, and we instructed the guests on arm exercises and core work. I blasted the music and tried to lose myself in the workout and not focus on Erik's intense glare.

"Okay. For the last fifteen minutes, we're going to just swim. Have fun with it," I shouted. Some ladies did hand-stands, some did body waves, but Erik torpedoed around the pool. After a few minutes, he flipped on his back and executed a perfect backstroke. His hands sliced through the water like blades as the sunlight highlighted his sculpted chest.

Isa swam up beside me. "Damn, you don't have a chance."

And she was right. I didn't have a chance of resisting this Triton.

5

ERIK

At the end of class, I hopped up on the side of the pool next to my mom and sister.

Holly shook her head. "I can't believe you put on a tail. You are so lame."

"Not a big deal. SEAL, merman, frogman, Triton. Same thing."

My sister punched my arm. "You like Aria, don't you?"

"What's not to like? She's beautiful and a champion."

My mom gave me an approving grin. "Oh, Erik. You should ask her out on a proper date. She's lovely. I worry about you on your deployments. It would be nice if you settled down and came home to a loving wife."

There my mom went. A true romantic. She never recovered after my father passed away. But they had shown me the meaning of true love and made me hopeful that one day I would find that myself. Fuck the SEAL ninety-five percent divorce rate. When I got married, it would be forever. My mom used to tell me the most important decision I would ever make in my life wasn't what job I would take, but who I would marry. I took her advice to heart.

Aria swam over to us, her smoking hot body glistening from the water. I wanted to rip off that bikini top with my teeth and suck on her nipples until she begged me to fuck her.

"Thank you all for coming. Holly, your arm movements are great."

"Oh, thank you." She bit her nails, and I could tell my sister was nervous. "I hate to ask you this but since you are in town, are you giving any lessons?"

"I didn't have any planned, but I'd be happy to coach you. Would you like me to look at your routine?"

My sister's eyes lit up. "Oh my god. You wouldn't mind? I'd love that."

I took a deep breath, and let it out slowly. Here was my moment. I normally didn't hesitate when asking out a girl, and I certainly wasn't afraid of being rejected in front of my family. I was a SEAL, for fuck's sake, and wasn't afraid of anything, but for some inexplicable reason this girl tied me up in knots. It was a feeling that was foreign to me.

"Can I take you out tonight? I'll show you around Coronado."

Aria's eyes darted between me and my mom's hopeful face. Her lip twisted probably since I had backed her into a corner.

"Sure. That sounds like fun."

Score.

I felt a tinge of guilt asking her out in front of my family, knowing that she probably didn't feel like she could say no, but I got what I'd come for.

A date with this beautiful, sexy woman.

"Great. I'll pick you up here at five."

"Okay. See you then. Holly, take off your tail and follow me."

They both wiggled off their tails and without a backward glance, Aria swam out toward the middle of the pool with Holly following closely behind.

My mom also removed her tail and stood up. "Well, that was nice of her to work with Holly. She seems so sweet.

And an Olympian—what a catch! Where are you going to take her? I could make reservations at Addison."

Whoa, mom. Addison was the fanciest restaurant in town. I planned to spoil Aria, but a stuffy old-school restaurant wasn't my scene. "I got this, Ma, but thanks."

"I remember my first date with your father. I was so nervous. I must've tried on twenty dresses. But he brought me flowers, and we had the best night."

Her eyes sparkled when she talked about my father. True love. I yearned for that. I'd done my fair share of womanizing since I'd been a SEAL. Hell, at Annapolis my yearbook said, "Erik was known for his love of fast cars and faster women." But after this last deployment, I wanted to find a partner, someone to miss me when I was gone.

The few SEAL marriages I'd seen that worked all involved incredibly strong and independent women. Women who had goals and identities beyond being just a Team wife.

She dried off, put on a cover up, and sat on a lounge chair, watching Holly. I wrapped myself in my towel and changed out of my tail and put my board shorts back on.

I grabbed my keys and waved goodbye to my mom, my sister, and Aria. Aria waved back, and I jogged down the beach to work. I couldn't wait for our date tonight.

6

ARIA

My breath came in short spurts as I leaned against my front door. Done. I had just completed my daily pre-BUD/S regimen. A two-mile ocean swim, a four-mile fast paced run, and a series of pushups, pullups, squats, lunges, and sit-ups. My legs quivered and my shins burned. But I knew that this workout was a piece of cake compared to what torture would await me in BUD/S. Training for the Olympics had been rigorous, but people had believed in me. And I had been training alongside women. This time, everyone would expect me to fail. And I'd be the lone woman in a sea of men.

I opened my front door and collapsed on the sofa as Flounder ran over to lick the salty sweat off my face. The urge to hobble over to the tub and take an Epsom bath tempted me. But I had to get ready for my date with Erik.

My *date*. How strange that word sounded. Dating was for other girls—I just had meaningless hookups. My head ached, but I couldn't tell if it was from exercising under the warm San Diego sun or from nervousness about tonight. Erik was gorgeous, cocky for sure, but as Isa had pointed out, he seemed sweet for bringing his family. Why would he put in so much effort to go out with me?

Maybe he had an ulterior motive.

In the past, men had pretended they were interested in me. Only later had I found out that they wanted to use me to endorse their products or be a spokesperson for their company. It was easier for me to believe he wanted something from me than to believe that a man that hot could actually be interested in getting to know me. Me, not just the gold medal winner, but Aria, just Aria.

I hoped for the best and tumbled into the shower like a drunk trying to sober up. Remind me why I was doing this to myself again? What drove me to this compulsion to want to always be the best? Sometimes I scared myself—I had the tunnel vision of a serial killer.

As the warm water beaded against my flesh, I exhaled. The watermelon scent of my shampoo filled the steam, forcing my nerves to calm down. I emerged from the shower, dried my body, and slathered myself up in cocoa butter.

I dropped my towel and stood naked in front of the mirror. My stomach turned when I saw my freckled skin, flat chest, boyish hips, and toned arms. I felt like Carrie in that horror movie. Maybe his interest in me was some cruel joke.

The ring of my phone jolted me out of my insecurity.

"Hi, Mom."

"Hi, Aria. How are you?"

"Good." I paused.

Did I dare mention to her that I am going on a date?

I wasn't in the mood to be lectured about how men were only after one thing and would only stop me from achieving my goals.

"Good? Nothing will be good until you give up this ridiculous idea of becoming a SEAL. I don't understand you, throwing away all your lucrative endorsements. You could be the star of Cirque de Soleil or a coach at top college, but instead, you pursue a life of poverty. You may be intelligent, but you have no common sense."

I didn't have the time for her nagging. I'd heard it all before.

"I got to go."

"Why? What do you have going on that's more important than talking to me?"

I felt almost nauseous as I spit the words out. "Actually, I have a date tonight."

"A date? With who? You have only been there a few days. Are you on one of those dating apps where men swipe women for hookups? I told you not to put your picture on those. You are a celebrity. It would be a public relations nightmare if someone screenshotted you. It's pretty desperate if you ask me."

God, did she ever let up? "No, mom. I'm not on Tinder. I met this guy named Erik. He's a SEAL. He invited me out and—"

"On a date? Why would a SEAL want to date you? I thought they were attracted to feminine girls."

I gulped. I didn't need this right now. "Thanks, Mom."

"Oh, honey. That's not what I meant. You are strong and fierce, but you should be suspicious of his motives. You are a champion. He could be using you for your connections. There are so many beautiful women in San Diego. You need to ask yourself—why would he want me?"

My lungs constricted, making it hard to breathe. "How can you say those things to me? Why is it so hard for you to believe that a man would be interested in me?"

"Honey, I didn't say no man would be interested in you. I just questioned a Navy SEAL's intentions. Your decisions in life affect me, too. I didn't sacrifice my happiness and goals for you to give up on yours to go chasing a man."

My heart accelerated. "I'm not chasing a man, Mother. He asked me out. And I'm going. Plus, I won an Olympic gold medal. How am I not achieving my goals? I just ran four miles in twenty-eight minutes in boots and swam two miles in the ocean. Just leave me alone and live your own life."

"Don't you talk that way to me, missy. I gave up everything for you. I didn't date. I worked three jobs, and I never spent any money on myself. I organized BINGO nights to fundraise for your synchro club. All for your dreams and your goals."

"I never asked you to do that. That was your choice. You cut my father out of your life, never even telling him you were pregnant. He didn't even know I existed. And thanks to you, he never will. And these were your goals. I was four! What did I know about synchro? Bye, mom."

I hung up the phone and tried to push away the cruelty of her words. My face, neck, and ears seemed impossibly hot.

I had sacrificed my life too. As fearless as I pretended to be, I was scared to death of doing anything that jeopardized my success, including having a personal life. What about what I had given up?

As tears streamed down my face, a realization hit me.

I needed to spend some time on nurturing Aria the woman instead of just focusing on Aria the athlete.

I made a vow to make a change in my life.

I found a matching lavender lace bra and panty set and slipped them on my body. Next, I applied my makeup, softer than I did for competitions, spritzed on perfume, and blew dry my hair. My polish bottle beckoned me, and I spent the next half an hour painting my nails. Once they had dried, I walked over to the closet and debated my clothing choices. I didn't want to overdress. I picked out the sexiest, casual outfit I could find—a strappy, aqua tank top and white linen shorts. I slipped my feet into some cute brand new tennis shoes.

A floating sensation overtook me like all my burdens had been lifted. I took another glance in the mirror. But this time, I didn't see a hardened Olympian. I saw a sexy, feminine woman.

And I couldn't wait to get to know her.

7

ERIK

T he rest of the day dragged, and I was counting down the minutes until I was off. A glimpse of the sun informed me that my commander would soon be excusing us. After six months in BUD/S, I could accurately tell time by looking at the shade of the sky, the brightness of the sun, and the position of the moon. The second we were dismissed, I showered again and dabbed on some cologne. I always kept some civilian clothes on base, so I changed into a black T-shirt and cargo shorts. I walked back to the Del, purchased some flowers, and awaited Aria.

Ten minutes later, she entered the pool area. Her red hair skimmed her mid back, and her natural beauty stood out in this sea of So Cal blondes. On this warm summer night, she wore a skimpy tank top and short shorts that hit right at her mid-thighs. I could see the outline of her panties under her clothes, and I was dying to take them off and lick her until she came for me. But I had to go slow tonight. I didn't want a one-night stand with her. I wanted to get her to date me, trust me, and maybe she would help me with my business.

I walked over and grinned down at her. "You look beautiful. These are for you."

"Oh, thanks. They are lovely." Her eyes darted around me, and she pulled her hair and rubbed her hands down her clothes. I could tell she was nervous which I found adorable. "Where are we headed?"

"To Leroy's. It's a restaurant down the street." I offered her my arm, and she took it, her tiny hand sliding on my bicep. On television, she had looked so lithe, but up close I could see how perfectly sculpted her muscles were, especially her ass. Some guys liked skinny girls, but I thought Aria had the perfect body. Firm and tight. I imagined fucking her from behind with my hands gripped on her tight booty.

We strolled down Orange Avenue amongst the tourists in this picturesque coastal town. I was proud to have her on my arm and to enjoy this peaceful moment in paradise, knowing that next month, I'd be deployed in hell.

The hostess greeted us, and we sat at a table in the back. I scanned the menu.

Aria fidgeted in her seat, and I was shocked that the confident champion I'd watched on television was so shy in person.

The waitress came over to our table. "Hi. I'm Misty. What can I get for you?"

Aria spoke first. "I'll have the poke tacos and a blood orange Cosmo."

"And I'll have the burger, medium rare, and a Coronado Brew Mermaid Red Ale." I winked at Aria.

"Those will be right up."

Aria glared at me. "Interesting beverage choice."

I licked my lips. "I want to see what you taste like."

She swept her hair over her face, hiding behind her bangs. "So, did you always want to be a SEAL?"

"Yup. I swam for Annapolis, was commissioned as an officer, and then joined the Teams. But I've wanted to be a SEAL since I was a little boy. Actually, I was a competitive swimmer in high school."

"Oh, you swam? That's cool. What events?"

"IM and butterfly. I once dreamed of the Olympics, but my parents couldn't afford for me to move away from home and train. And even if they could've, I don't think they would've let me. They wanted me to have a normal childhood."

She cringed at my words.

Fuck. Why had I said that?

"No, your parents were smart. I had no life at all. I was homeschooled, spent ten hours a day in the pool, never went to prom. I mean, I've never even had a boyfriend. My life kind of sucks."

Her words made me realize that my parents had been right. I knew the dedication it took to be an elite athlete, and I now agreed with them. That kind of life was incompatible with being a well-rounded kid.

"Seriously? You're joking. You're gorgeous. You didn't date anyone at Stanford?"

"No. I mean most of the athletes hook up with each other or fall into long-term relationships. But I never had the time nor had I ever actually shared a huge connection with anyone. I was on both the collegiate team and the USA Senior National team." She sighed. "My mind is warped. Like legit right now I feel guilty having dinner with you. I feel like I should be at home stretching or something."

I laughed. I'd never met a woman like her. My last girl-friend had no goals in life besides partying. If anyone could teach Aria to have a good time, it was me. "Since my little sister does synchro I know a bit about it. You probably can hold your breath underwater better than most SEALs."

She grinned, a devilish look on her face. "Not probably. Definitely."

I loved that she wasn't afraid to challenge me. "You think you can hold your breath longer than me?"

"I know I can. Let's make a bet. Winner buys loser dinner."

I shook my head. "Nope, sorry. I'm buying your dinner. And that's one bet I won't take. A couple of my buddies died at the bottom of the BUD/S pool in a breath-holding challenge. Neither one would quit."

Her face dropped. "Oh, that's awful. I'm sorry."

I closed my eyes and took a moment to remember my friends. "It's a hard job. Our training is life and death."

The waitress brought us our drinks, and I saw Devin and a few other SEALs walk into the restaurant. Devin shaped his fingers like a box and stuck his tongue out through the middle. I wanted to smack that mother fucker. Luckily, Aria didn't see him because she was facing away from them. My other buddies acknowledged me and sat at the bar, no doubt to get wasted. Aria must've noticed my reaction because she glanced in their direction but then quickly turned her attention back to me.

I downed my beer. "So, only in town a month? What do you have planned next? Are you trying to compete for the next Olympics?"

Her lips pressed together in a slight grimace. "Uh, not sure. I have so many opportunities I can't make up my mind."

I studied her face. She was lying to me. My gut told me a woman who had won a gold medal was anything but indecisive. But she didn't know me, and this was our first date. I would let it go for now.

"What do you want to do?"

She bit her lip. "I'm not sure exactly." Her gaze grew distant. "Did you grow up here?" she asked.

I noted her rapid subject change. "Yup. My dad was stationed here. He was a submariner. You?"

"Marin. Near San Francisco. I spent my whole life in California, but I think Coronado is the most beautiful town I've ever been in."

"Not as beautiful as you."

She blushed, and her green eyes seemed to turn a brighter hue. Our food arrived, and we spent the rest of dinner getting to know each other. When the check came, I quickly paid, and we left.

Normally, I always had a plan. But something about her

made me want to let her take the lead. "The night's still young. Are you up for an adventure?"

"Absolutely. I'm open to anything. Something active, outdoors. Let's enjoy the beautiful weather."

I loved how adventurous she was. My ex's idea of a good time was finding an Instagram-worthy place where she could pose while I took hundreds of pictures of her for her followers. What was the point of recording your life when you didn't take the time to live it?

"Okay. Let's grab my bike, and I'll rent you one. We can ride around the island during the sunset. It's an easy six miles."

She gritted her teeth and pursed her lips tight. "Let's just walk so we can stop in some shops also."

"The bike path is really the best way to see Coronado. It's probably one of the best bike routes in the country."

"I'd prefer to walk."

"Okay." I didn't want to press, but her reluctance baffled me.

I wasn't ready to end this night. I thought of the typical places to take her—moonlit stroll on the beach, cocktails at the Del, or even a ride on the Coronado gondola. But nothing seemed perfect for Aria. I needed to wow her if there was any hope of getting her to help me ensnare my clients in a few weeks.

Then it hit me. Something unique, powerful, and breathtaking.

Just like her.

My hand reached to hers, and I wrapped my fingers around her palm. "I want to show you something."

"Where are you taking me?"

"To the Naval Special Warfare Base."

Her mouth widened into a grin but I wasn't sure why. Maybe she was excited to get on base. I remembered the first time I set foot on the BUD/S compound a desire to be the best overtook me. Maybe her pride as an Olympian compelled her to feel the same. We walked a few more blocks, past the Del and back to base. I flashed my ID at the gate and led her inside.

Her eyes widened like saucers as a group of BUD/S candidates raced by her. Those sorry fuckers probably hadn't seen a woman in months. Just her scent alone must've driven them insane.

Their instructor, my buddy Pat, must've caught the destination of their gazes. "Do you think you fuckers are worthy to even look at a SEAL's woman?"

"No, Instructor Walsh," they yelled in unison.

Ha. Control, Pat had complete control over them. Pretty soon, it would be my turn to be their master.

We walked past the men, and I led her to the beach over-looking the "O" Course. A group of SEAL trainees was practicing its obstacles. We sat on the sand. The competing sounds of cars whizzing by on the nearby road and the crash of the waves against the shore stirred in my head.

"Wow. This is so cool! Thank you for bringing me here. I've read about the course and seen videos, but it's so awesome to see up close."

"Thought you would like it. I became a man on this course. It's harder than it looks." I pointed to my nemesis. "That fucking obstacle, Dirty Name, almost cost me my Trident. It doesn't look that challenging, but if you don't jump at the right angle, you are screwed."

She exhaled. "Well, I'd love to try it."

Ha. That would be the day when a woman could master our course. Even an athlete like Aria. "If you're a good girl, I'll let you take a crack at it some time."

She licked her lips and leaned into me. "But what if I'm a bad girl?"

"Then I'll definitely let you try it." My hand moved slowly

through her windblown hair, and her head tilted. I leaned in as the sunset beckoned me to her lips. Claiming her hot sweet mouth, my tongue tangled with hers, and she tasted like pure bliss.

It was the type of kiss that could get me through a long deployment.

I'd kissed many women in my life, but something told me that this would be a lip lock that I would remember for the rest of my life.

8

ARIA

Everything about this night had been heavenly. From the crunchy taco shells which cradled the perfectly seasoned poke, the tangy punch of my blood orange Cosmo, to this moonlit stroll with my handsome date. But Erik had upped the ante.

He had granted me access to the place I dreamt about every night—where I would be spending six months of my life.

The coveted SEAL base. I had been this close to the "O" Course. He had even promised that he would let me try it.

And that kiss. It was like one of those mythical first kisses that you read about in books or saw in movies. Perfectly choreographed. His lips had been soft, but his grip on my neck had been firm. He was sweet yet rough, loving yet forceful, innocent yet dirty. Oh so dirty.

But instead of enjoying this blissful moment, my stomach lurched in guilt.

I hadn't been honest with him.

His hand caressed the front of my tank top, and he gently thumbed my nipple through the fabric. "Let's go back to my place. I live in a condo overlooking the base."

Every part of me wanted to scream yes. Go home with this sexy hunk. I imagined him throwing me over his back like some caveman and fucking me until I couldn't stop coming.

"I can't. I have to get home, walk my dog, and go to sleep. I teach tomorrow at eight, and I need to wake up early so I can put in a three-hour workout before class." The second those words left my mouth I realized how ridiculous they sounded.

"You're crazy. The only people I know who work out that long are SEALs."

And those training to be SEALs. "And Olympians," I countered. *Good save.*

He nodded. "Spend the night with me, and I'll work out with you."

My body posture perked up. That would be great! He could fuck me all night, and then in the morning we could run, do an ocean swim, and maybe he'd let me try the "O" course.

But that wouldn't be fair to him. If I was going to hook up with this man, I had to tell him my plans. "I have to decline. But I've had a great time tonight. This has been the best date I've ever had. But I really do have to go."

I stood up and brushed the sand off my shorts, the ocean breeze flipping down the strap of my tank top, revealing my bra. Erik grinned as his gaze dropped to my breasts. I pulled up the strap and laughed, grateful that I wasn't wearing a dress. I remembered the scene in the Marilyn Monroe movie, *Seven Year Itch*. She had filmed *Some Like It Hot* on this very beach. I loved being here, surrounded by history.

Pulling me to him, he gently cradled my cheek in his palm. "Can I see you tomorrow night?"

Dammit, Aria. This guy was great. Super hot, sexy, smart. "What did you have in mind?"

"Wonder Woman is playing at the local theater. Let me take you."

Wonder Woman? I was dying to see that flick. She was an Amazonian warrior who could fight alongside men.

And this would be a perfect way to gauge how receptive Erik would be about female Navy SEALs.

"I'd love to."

"Okay. Give me your phone."

I reached into my purse and handed him my phone. He entered his number and then called his phone, thus getting my number. "I'll text you and let you know what time it starts. Let me walk you home."

No. I wasn't ready for that. I couldn't resist him being that close to my bed. "I'm fine. It's a beautiful night."

He took my hand. "Aria, I insist. You are beautiful. Some guy could grab you."

And I could protect myself. "I feel safe in this tourist town."

"Fine. But I have to walk you off base."

I agreed, and he walked me off base and back in front of the Del.

He leaned down and gave me another kiss. This one was sweeter than the last one but still laced with urgency. Like a magnet, I fought to separate my body from his, our attraction pulling us together.

"Good night, Erik."

"Good night, Aria."

As I walked through the picturesque Coronado Village, I marveled at my luck. So far, Erik had behaved like a perfect gentleman, and I didn't suspect he had some ulterior motive as my mom believed. Maybe he could be the right guy for me after all. "Everything happens for a reason," my hippy mother used to say when she was pretending that she was so spiritual and kind. Maybe Erik had been sent to me, to guide me through this path. Maybe he would accept my goals and help me reach them.

Either way, I would know soon. I planned to tell him tomorrow. If he was the right guy for me, he would understand my dreams and support them.

9

ERIK

I slept in, appreciating a rare Saturday off. As a SEAL, I worked most weekends. I enjoyed a leisurely breakfast, got a quick workout in, and then hit the shower to get ready for my evening with Aria.

I met Aria outside the Village theater at six o'clock. She was wearing khaki shorts and a violet tank top. Her long hair was loose and wavy. She looked like a goddess.

I flashed my phone to show the two tickets, and we went inside the theater. We ordered popcorn and drinks and found our seats.

I put my arm around Aria, and she rested her head on my chest.

"Thanks for inviting me. I can't wait to see this."

The movie started, and I was blown away by the scenery. But nothing impressed me more than Diana Prince's complete badassery.

But Aria seemed to love the movie even more than I had. Every time Diana defeated someone, Aria squeezed my hand. When the movie was over, and we walked out of the theater, Aria's face beamed.

"Oh my god. That movie was so incredible. Don't you think? I loved it. Diana was so powerful and strong. She'd make a great SEAL."

Ha. "Yeah, she would. Too bad, she doesn't exist."

Aria's mouth stretched into a wide grin. I hadn't seen her look this happy since I'd met her, even when she was in the water.

I was about to suggest a stroll on the beach, but Aria turned to me. "Let's go for a swim."

"Where?"

"In the ocean."

I paused. "I didn't bring my trunks."

She gave me a playful glance. "In that case, we will have to go au naturel."

Fuck yeah. "Sounds like a plan. I'll take you on base, and we can swim off our private beach. That way we won't get arrested."

We walked back to base, and I flashed my ID. It crossed my mind that I had swim shorts in my locker, but I decided to keep that to myself.

We then headed out past the obstacle course to a secluded part of the beach, covered by some rocks.

I stripped off my clothes, and she pulled off her top and shorts, revealing a matching white lace bra and panty set. Maintaining eye contact with me, she unhooked her bra, revealing her small but pert breasts. Then she slipped off her panties, and I confirmed that she was a natural redhead. I was shocked that she had seemed so shy yesterday, but now she dripped confidence. My eyes danced around her body. It was pure perfection. Her stomach had definition I'd only seen in fitness magazines, and her ass was round and tight. I stared at her beautiful pussy, waxed in a sexy triangle. My cock rose to attention. I had to fuck her.

"The water's cold," I warned.

"Fine by me." She ran in front of me on the beach into the water, and I chased after her. Once the waves hit her waist, she began to swim.

We swam out to the first buoy, and I was impressed at her

pace. Her strokes were even, and she didn't seem to choke on the salt water.

It was almost as if she had trained in the ocean. Who knew? Maybe open water swims were part of her regimen for the Olympics.

She was a few strides ahead of me, but I quickly caught up, barreling toward her, until I grabbed her by the waist and pulled her into me.

I pressed my body into hers and brushed a lock of hair out of her face. "You're a pretty amazing swimmer."

She blinked the salt water out of her eyes. "You're not bad yourself."

I felt her tremble in my arms, and I wasn't sure if it was from the chill of the water or the closeness of our naked bodies. I wanted to take her right then and there, fuck her in the ocean.

A wave rippled by and we bobbed in the water, but my arms remained around this beautiful woman who felt so tiny in my grasp.

I cupped her naked ass, and she wrapped her legs around my waist.

My cock was pressed hard against her thigh. It had always been a fantasy of mine to fuck in the water.

We kissed as we were treading water. Her pussy was so fucking close to my cock. I lifted her up to take one of her beautiful breasts in my mouth, sucking her nipple until she moaned.

My lips made their way up to her earlobe. "Babe, I'm clean. The Navy tests me thoroughly after every deployment, and I haven't been with anyone since my last test."

"Well, I'm on the pill, and I haven't been with anyone since I was last tested."

Fuck yeah. She didn't need to say anything else. I kept my legs in a steady eggbeater motion to stay afloat. I glided her onto my cock as I kissed her mouth. She was even tighter than I imagined. With one arm free to keep balance, my other arm guided her motion as her body rocked with the waves.

"This is so fucking hot, baby."

We were close enough to a place where I could stand on the ocean floor, so I lifted her off of me and swam with her until I could stand. Once my feet were firmly planted in the sand, I went to work on her nipples, kissing, teasing and sucking them. I wrapped her legs around me again and pounded her onto my cock.

I was mesmerized by her body. Even when I was fucking

her, she moved so gracefully, as if she was performing just for me.

The heat from her core kept me warm despite the frigid water.

"I could fuck you all night out here. I'm not going to come until you do."

She smiled as my hand gripped her ass, and she rubbed her clit against my crotch. Her breath came in gasps as I slammed her onto me, pushing her closer to ecstasy. She finally screamed out as I took her mouth with a kiss and I could feel her come undone. I let go inside her and came so hard.

Fuck, that was so incredible.

She climbed off of me with a cautious smile on her face.

"Want to go back to my place and spend the night?" I pointed to the high rise.

"Oh. I don't know if I'm ready to spend the night with you," she teased.

"Aria, we just fucked in the ocean. And I plan to fuck you all night."

"Okay, let's race. You beat me, and I'll spend the night at your place."

I loved how competitive she was. "You're on."

I gave her another kiss, and we swam back toward the shore.

I kept my gaze focused on her gorgeous ass as she swam in front of me. But when we were close to shore, I sped up and overtook her, though I had the feeling she let me win. Once we reached the beach, we ran out of the water, used my shirt as a towel, and then dressed.

I took her hand, and we walked along the shore, exited the base, and then entered my high rise. I loved my condo—it had views of the Del and the Naval Special Warfare base. I could roll out of bed and walk to work.

I pressed the button for the elevator, and once inside, I pinned her to the wall for another kiss. She tasted salty and hot.

When the elevator door opened again, an older couple greeted us. My breath hitched—the man resembled my father. But I knew that I would never see him again. Not in this lifetime.

I opened the door to my place, and Aria took in the view. Her clothes were still damp. "You want to change? I can give you some clothes."

"No, I'm good. I'm used to being wet."

Fuck yeah. I pulled her into me. "Come here, baby, and let me taste you."

I caressed her face and kissed her again. Inhaling her unique, feminine scent, slowly exploring her mouth with my tongue, urging her closer to me. My cock shot to attention. I was dying to part her firm thighs, spread her legs, and eat her pussy. Her hand traced the outline of my biceps, before resting on my chest. My arms closed around her lower back as I blew kisses on her earlobes, tasted her sweet skin, and buried my head in her cleavage.

She kissed me back and began to relax her body as my cock pressed against her.

I couldn't wait to taste her any longer.

I stripped off her clothes, picked her up and propped her ass on the back of my sofa.

"Spread your legs, baby."

She tossed her hair back and spread her legs so wide I couldn't believe it. I knelt in front of her with my knees on the couch and inhaled her scent, salty and sweet. Kissing her delicate folds, teasing her with my mouth, I took one long lick down her center, and she gasped.

"Just what I thought. You taste better than Mermaid's Red."

She laughed.

But one lick wasn't enough to satisfy me.

I wrapped her legs around my neck and licked her gold medal pussy, drunk on her sweetness. She moaned when I gripped her thighs and pulled her tighter against my mouth. I couldn't get enough of her.

"Come for me, champ. Come all over my face."

I sucked on her clit and slid my finger inside her. I could feel her tense and release, and I knew she was so fucking close. She reached down and grasped my hair, urging me into her as I devoured her. She let out a scream as she came so hard her body contracted.

"That's my girl."

I pulled her to my side, wrapped my arm around her and cuddled with her on the sofa. We gazed out at the ocean, and she leaned into me.

I felt a twinge of guilt that I had initially pursued her partially because I wanted her to help me with my business. But now, it was more than that. My insides twisted when I was around her, and I sometimes felt nervous in her presence—which had never happened to me before.

She sighed, gazing at the ocean. "This is the most incredible view. I've never seen anything so beautiful in my entire life."

I looked right at her. "Neither have I."

10

ARIA

I woke the next morning, and it took me a few minutes to remember where I was. But the Coronado sunrise quickly reminded me that I was in Erik's bed. But unfortunately, he wasn't in it.

My chest constricted as I recalled my previous drunken hookups, waking up alone, filled with regret. I completely owned my choices for having casual sex, but no matter how much I had tried to convince myself that I actually had enjoyed sex with my previous lovers, honestly it had never been that satisfying, physically or emotionally.

But last night with Erik had been different. The sex had been mind blowing. I'd never come with a lover before. But more than the physical chemistry, I'd felt that we had connected on a deeper level.

My entire life, I had always figured that people pretended

to like me because of my accomplishments. But Erik seemed to actually be interested in who I was as a person.

The only problem was that I didn't exactly know who Aria the woman was. Aria the champion always had dominated her.

I hurried out of bed, pulled on my clothes, and went into the kitchen where Erik was making breakfast.

I gasped at the sight of him, wearing nothing but long pajama bottoms which hung low on his waist, giving me a view of his happy trail. His chest was ripped, and his shoulders were broad.

He brushed his dark hair out of his face. "Morning, beautiful."

"Morning." I couldn't believe he thought I was beautiful. My mom's words filled my head with doubts. I imagined that Erik would date a beach babe with sun-kissed hair and pouty lips.

"You hungry?"

"Sure." Another first. I'd spent the night with a man, and now he was cooking for me. I pinched myself to make sure I wasn't dreaming.

He handed me a plate filled with sunny side up eggs, thick

cut bacon, and toast. He sat next to me with his own plate and poured us both some coffee.

His eyes brightened as he checked me out. "What are your plans today?"

I didn't dare tell him. My plans had included preparing for BUD/S: an ocean swim, a beach run, and pushups until I collapsed. You know, a typical Sunday.

"Oh, just a long workout. You?"

"Do you ever take a day off?"

I shook my head. "Not even the day after I took gold."

"You're more hardcore than I am. But I play hard, too." He reached across the table and held my hand. "Spend the day with me, babe. We can relax, go biking, or drive up the coast. I can show you some of the cool hidden beach towns."

Biking, ha. He would laugh at me when he found out I'd never ridden a bicycle. "That sounds fun." My gut twisted. I liked Erik and didn't want to deceive him. I had vowed to tell him the truth after we had seen Wonder Woman, but we had been caught up in the moment. But now, there was no excuse. I had to confess my plans and see what he had to say about females being in the Teams. Maybe he would be completely supportive and help me train.

I took a deep breath and eased in. "I read that SEALs are going to let in the first woman soon. What do you think about that?"

He dropped my hand, took a sip of his coffee, and gave me a keen look. "I think it's the dumbest fucking idea ever."

Well so much for him being supportive. I knew I should've dropped the topic. I had wanted to know his position on the issue, and it was evident he was against it.

Move on, Aria. He's a great guy with a typical SEAL mindset. Just shut your mouth and— "Really? Why?"

Dammit. The feminist in me couldn't be quiet.

"Because no woman could pass BUD/S, first of all. The Navy will end up lowering its standards, and good men will die because of it. I'm sick of all this politically correct bullshit. Ideas implemented by legislators who have frankly never served a day in their fucking lives in any branch of the military, let alone special operations."

Alrighty then. Tell me how you really feel. "Okay. But I mean, what *if* a woman could pass BUD/S, without lowering the standards. Someone like Wonder Woman. I've met some athletes who could. I knew this one woman Kendall, a wrestler, who could totally do it. She was so strong and fierce."

"Wonder Woman is fictional." He shook his head. "It's

impossible. It's not just about strength, though that's a huge part of it. It's about endurance. No woman can perform the same physical tasks as a man without the standards being lowered. It has never happened and it never will."

Watch me. "It has never happened because no woman has ever been able to try. And what if a woman could pass? Then you still think she shouldn't be let in?"

"No. She shouldn't. It would ruin unit cohesion."

The hairs on the back of my neck stood straight up. "So are you saying that a woman couldn't pass BUD/S, or are you saying that a woman could pass BUD/S but then still shouldn't be a SEAL?"

He gave me a hard glare. "I'm saying that we are the most elite special operations force in the world. I'm not talking about women serving in the military. I'm talking about women serving in combat units. In theory, it's great, and I support women's rights to do any job. But academics and politicians can't understand the special operations battle-field. If a woman were captured by the enemy, she would be raped and tortured. If you have a small SEAL unit and the men are competing for the attraction of a female, it will take the focus off the mission."

I wanted to yell at him, but couldn't clue him into my vested personal interest in this topic. "That's ridiculous. I assume you don't think gay men should be in the SEALs either?"

"Why does everyone compare gender to sexual orientation? You are wrong. I have no problem with gay SEALs. In fact, I have two buddies in the Teams who are gay. But they are on separate Teams and would never have a relationship during a mission."

"But a woman can't control herself? Or you guys can't control yourselves around a woman?"

"It's biology. I wanted to fuck you the moment I saw you. So did my friend. If you were on my Team, all my buddies would want to fuck you too. It would distract from our mission. Not to mention the spouses of my Teammates wouldn't be happy to know that a female was serving alongside their husbands on long combat missions. Sometimes we spend months living in the middle of fucking nowhere in a dirt hole."

I stared at him, disgusted by his answers. Why had I slept with this asshole? I had been wrong. We had nothing in common at all. If all SEALs thought as he did, I was in for a challenge even rougher than I imagined.

He placed his hand on mine, but I retracted from his grasp. "Sorry. I get worked up about this. There isn't even a woman in the BUD/S pipeline, so we don't have to worry about this debate for a while."

Ha. There is too a woman in the pipeline, buddy. You are looking right at her.

I sulked like a child—pushing my food around with my fork on the plate. I couldn't even look at this guy. I needed to get out of here. Get some clear air before I lost it.

His arm reached out to touch mine across the table. I snapped it away.

"What's wrong? Are you that upset about my opinion?"

"It's disappointing. That's all."

He stood up and tried to pull me out of my chair but resisted. "Let's not ruin the day over this. We can agree to disagree."

No, we can't. Next January, you will learn the truth. My name will be plastered all over the newspapers. As the first female in BUD/S.

I stood up to leave. "Thanks for breakfast. I need to get going and walk my dog."

He ground his teeth and glared at me. "Fine."

I grabbed my purse, walked out the door, and pressed the elevator button.

Ever since I'd met him, he seemed like so much more. He was sweet with his family, had been kind and patient with me, and had seemed genuinely interested in getting to know me. So far, there was no indication that he was using me for anything. I felt like we had truly connected on more than just a physical level. I thought about him every day last week. He had made me feel beautiful and desirable and not a bit like the awkward dork I saw myself as. And I had been charmed by his laid back yet masculine So-Cal surfer boy charm.

I shouldn't have gone on a date with Erik. He was nothing but a typical chauvinistic pig. He had been nothing but a distraction.

A completely drop dead gorgeous, mind blowing, orgasm-giving distraction.

I refused to allow myself to be sidelined from my dreams by a man.

11

ERIK

She slammed the door behind her. Fuck. What the fuck had just happened? Why would she get so pissed off about my opinion on women in combat?

We'd had such a great first date, and our second date had been incredible too. I actually liked this girl. I didn't want this to be a one night stand.

My phone rang. I glanced at the screen. My mom. Great.

"Hey, Ma."

"Hi, Erik. I was just calling to find out how your date the other night went."

Most of my Teammates would think I was pathetic for confiding in my mom. But after my father passed away, we'd become very close.

"Not good."

She let out a sigh. "What happened?"

"It was so stupid. We saw Wonder Woman, and we were having a good time . . ." I paused because I was definitely *not* going to fill her in on the sordid details, "but then she asked what I thought about women in combat."

"Oh Erik, you didn't tell her, did you?"

"Of course I did."

"You realize she's an Olympic Gold medalist. An over-achiever. I'm sure she believes a woman can do anything a man can do."

"That's not the point, Ma. I'm not going to lie about my beliefs just to impress a girl. I don't think women should be SEALs. If she doesn't want to see me again because of who I am then that's that."

"Oh well, that's a shame, I think she would've been good for you. You know, your father and I didn't agree about everything. I believe the best partnerships are between two people who complement and challenge each other, not who are clones of each other."

"Yeah, well she stormed off, so that's that."

"I'm sure she's just disappointed, that's all. You should reach out to her if you are still interested in her."

"I'll think about it."

We talked a bit more and then said goodbye.

Dammit. My mom was probably right, but it didn't matter. Aria walked out. Even though we had only had two dates and I barely knew her, I had felt that we'd had the potential to start a relationship. Aria had probably been the wise one when she had turned me down initially for a date. She didn't live here, was only in town for three more weeks and I was about to deploy for at least six.

Still, there was a knot in my chest that had not been there before.

Get over it, Anderson. Stop being a pussy. It's done.

I needed to get out of here, clear my head. After taking a quick shower, I got dressed and decided to head up the coast. Instead of staying on Orange Ave., I drove down Ocean Ave., appreciating the view of the multi-million dollar homes. When I turned my head toward the shoreline, I saw Aria, running along the beach with a beagle, just as she had said she was going to.

Damn, what drove her? I wondered if she wanted to defend her title in three years. Despite our difference of opinions and my residual anger toward her for bailing without so much as a backward glance, I couldn't shake the feeling that we would be perfect for each other. Waking up next to her had felt so right, and I hadn't once felt the desire to kick her out of my bed like I normally did after sex. Aria shared my passion and drive. Women I'd dated in the past could never understand my dedication to the Teams. I doubted Aria would ever question why I had to train so much.

I would be proud to show her off to my friends. Team guys always had a sort of competition amongst each other on who had the best girlfriend. Aria would win hands down.

And with her by my side, I just know I could make TritonFix a success.

I crossed the Coronado Bridge. Maybe my mom had been right; I had been insensitive. Aria wasn't a SEAL. She couldn't possibly understand the pressures of my job and how those stresses would be exacerbated by the addition of women to the Teams. It had been a stupid argument, and I had fallen right into it. There had been no correct way to answer her questions.

I would give her some space, but I refused to let a woman that fantastic walk out of my life without a fight.

12

ARIA

I soaked my aching muscles in the bathtub. I was so angry at myself for walking out on Erik yesterday. He had expressed his opinion, and I should've been more mature. Instead, I had stormed out like a petulant child who didn't get her way. What the hell had I expected? Of course, SEALs didn't think women should join the Teams. I knew this. I'd poured over hundreds of articles written by SEALs debating on whether women should be allowed in combat before I had ever made the decision to try.

These men had never seen a woman graduate from BUD/S. By nature, any man who became a SEAL had to be stubborn and unwilling to give up. It would be hard for these men to accept what they believed was a blow to their culture, their ethos, their way of life. The only way these SEALs would accept change was to have it thrust in their face.

If I had only kept my mouth shut, I could've spent more time with Erik. Had a hot summer affair to give me something to remember while I went through training.

But it wasn't just the sex, though it was by far the best sex of my life. The type of sex I'd only read about in romance novels. Something about Erik brought out another part of me. When I was with him, I wasn't focused on winning, or becoming a SEAL. I was actually having fun despite myself.

I should call him and apologize. But what was the point? I only had three more weeks left here, and then I would go to Officer Candidate School. Erik and I had no chance. He would never support my dreams. He had made that point loud and clear last night.

Today was going to be super awkward because I had promised to coach Erik's sister. He had asked me out in front of her and their mom, so I was sure that by now Holly already knew about our disastrous second date. I emerged from the tub, dried off with a towel, and put my swimsuit on under my sweats.

I turned to Flounder. "I'll take you to the beach when I get back."

Once in my car, I drove away from Coronado, over the bridge, toward a town called Poway. Thirty minutes later, I was completely shocked about how different this place seemed from coastal Coronado. The beautiful mountains beckoned me, and I was charmed by the rural landscape. I passed a high school and wondered if Erik had attended there.

Damn, why couldn't I get him out of my head? He'd gotten under my skin without me even realizing it.

I pulled outside of a charming one level ranch house. It seemed private, peaceful and serene, the exact opposite of the tiny apartment I'd grown up in. I scanned the driveway and saw only one car. Was it Erik's? My heart hammered in my chest. Omg . . . what if he was here? No. It was Monday. He was surely at work. And he probably never wanted to see me again.

I could hardly blame him after the way I'd treated him.

Taking a deep, bolstering breath, I rang the doorbell, and Holly answered the door. She was so pretty—she shared Erik's dark hair and blue eyes.

"Hi. Thank you for coming. Please come in."

"My pleasure." I walked inside and was immediately impressed by their home. Pictures were everywhere. Family portraits, Erik's little league shots, and a framed snap of him graduating from BUD/S, his handsome father standing beside him.

I'd had two dates with Erik and had slept with him, but there was so much more I didn't know about him. Was he close to his father? He had only mentioned him once to me —that he had been stationed on submarines.

But it was probably best that we hadn't shared more intimate conversations since we had no future. I definitely didn't want to open up to him about my fucked-up family.

Holly followed my gaze. "Oh, these. That was such a happy day. My dad was so proud of him. My father died of a heart attack a few weeks later."

"Oh no, that's awful."

"Yeah. My mom was a mess. Really fell apart. Erik really stepped up and took care of us."

A lump rose in my throat. I felt like such a bitch. Erik was a great guy, and I had totally thrown away an opportunity to get to know him. Why oh why had I let my temper get the best of me?

She led me outside to their pool which was surrounded by a huge back yard filled with dozens of citrus trees.

Holly and I dove into the pool and did a few laps to warm up. She then showed me her routine, which was impressive. I couldn't help but think that she needed to move up north if she was serious about synchro.

"Have you thought about moving to Marin to train with the Mermaids?"

"Of course! It would be my dream. I begged my parents when I was twelve, but they refused to split up the family. I'm not going to lie—I resented them. I always wonder how good I could've been if I'd lived near the top synchro club." She sighed. "My coach is great, but it's not the same. But my father really wanted both Erik and me to be kids, socialize with our friends and not become too focused on our sports. You know, Erik was an amazing swimmer. Could've probably swum at a national level. But he chose to follow my dad's footsteps and attend Annapolis."

"No. I didn't know that. Your parents were probably right. I never had any balance in my life. I was consumed by competing."

"Yeah. . . I was really furious at them for years," Holly admitted. "I felt like they were holding me back. But once my father died, I was so grateful for spending all that family time with him. Now, I just dream of being on the Stanford team. I'll be a senior next year, and I just hope I get accepted."

"Well, I can put you on the radar for the coach. She's really awesome. She takes most of her team from the Marin Mermaids, the Santa Clara Aquamaids, and the Walnut Creek Aquanuts. But she's always on the lookout for fresh talent. I'm here for a month if you want to work together."

Her face lit up. "Oh my god. Really? You are the best. I

never thought I'd see you again after today. I mean, well, because—oh I hope you don't mind, but my brother told my mom that you probably weren't going to go out on another date."

Awkward. "No, it's fine. I'll totally train you. Your brother is a great man. We had some fun dates. I'm just only going to be here for three more weeks, and then I'll be away."

"Oh, I know. Sorry to meddle. I just think you are so cool. Erik's been single for a while, and he seems to really like you. He deploys so much he's never around enough to get to know anyone."

A pang went through me. Why had I never thought about that? In a way, being a SEAL would be even harder on relationships than being an Olympian. Sure, I had competed around the world, but I would be gone for a week or so—SEALs deployed for months.

I now realized we had something else in common besides our work ethic. Loneliness. Erik had to get lonely despite being surrounded by his Teammates on missions. I wonder if he felt as cut off from the world as I did when I trained.

I turned my focus back to Holly. We worked on flexibility and breath control, and I cleaned up a portion of her choreography. She had a beautiful natural style that, though rough, was more refreshing compared to the often over trained styles of the girls in my home club. After an hour, I gave her some homework and said goodbye. I was eager to leave before her mom came home from work.

As I drove back to Coronado, my mind returned to Erik. I remembered how good it felt to have him kiss me senseless, to feel his strong arms around me, to have his undivided attention.

I hated to face the ugly truth.

I had blown my chance with this amazing guy.

I yearned for a second chance with Erik. I still had three weeks in town, and I wished I could spend it getting to know him.

13

ERIK

F riday rolled around again, and it had been a week since my first date with Aria. I'd done my best to not think about her, but every morning when I swam in the ocean, I remembered how incredible it had felt to fuck her out in the water. She was wild and uninhibited.

But she had surprisingly meant more to me than just great sex. On the surface, she portrayed herself as strong and confident. A badass woman. And she definitely had all of those qualities. But beneath her poised exterior, I'd seen a glimpse of her true self. She had an aching vulnerability that hid her shocking insecurities below her calm surface. These aspects of her character didn't turn me off. If anything, they drew me more to her. I felt that being with her would make me a better man—more driven, more focused. And I could help her too—teach her to have fun and stop being so hard on herself.

I wanted another chance with her.

I hit my workout hard and kept my eye on the time.

At eight thirty, I decided to take a run on the beach.

I ran up to the pool and watched Aria finish teaching her class with Isa, who was a cool woman, too. Her husband, Grady, was a legend—a Medal of Honor recipient. That badass had jumped on a bomb to save his fellow Marines. Now he was disfigured. But beautiful Isa, who had met and married him after his injuries, loved him anyway. One of the biggest fears for men in the Teams was that their wives would either cheat on them or leave them if they were injured. It was refreshing to meet a woman like Isa who loved her husband despite his appearance.

Aria smiled and cautiously waved when she saw me. She gathered and put away the equipment after her class, then emerged from the pool.

"I'm going to change really quick. I'll be right back."

I nodded, and she vanished with Isa. Ten minutes later, she walked over to me dressed in a tank top and shorts. Her hair hung in her face and she rubbed the back of her neck as she gave me a cautious, "Hi."

"Hey. Can I buy you a coffee?"

She nodded yes, and we walked over to the coffee cart outside the Del. She ordered a black coffee which surprised me because I was used to women ordering fancy lattes with foam art or those colorful, blended frozen concoctions for the sole purpose of memorializing the drink on Instagram. Another reminder of how unique she was.

I paid, and we sat at a small little table overlooking the ocean.

"I'm really sorry for walking out of your place the other morning," she blurted. "It wasn't fair ... to either of us. I got upset and should have stayed so we could talk things through."

She looked down at her feet, but I reached out to her and tilted her chin, forcing her to meet my eyes.

"Don't apologize. I get worked up when I talk about the Teams. It's my world. I've sacrificed so much of my life to become a SEAL, and I'm not allowed to talk about my job to anyone who is not in the Teams. There is so much I can't share with you, even if I wanted to." I blew out a breath, trying to keep my emotions in check. "I don't want to start a debate again, but no one has a clue what we go through in combat. Also, we brutalize each other in training. We spar, fight, and choke each other to learn how to protect ourselves from the enemy. I love women so much, and I can't imagine being so rough with a woman. Just trust me, allowing women on the Teams is really complicated."

She gave me a thoughtful glance. "I didn't know about the fighting during training. I've watched the full BUD/S documentary. I never saw that."

"Well, there is a whole bunch of training and hazing that goes on that we don't share with the world. I really can't talk about it."

She pursed her lips and seemed to understand. I decided to change the subject.

"Anyway, I hear you are working with my sister. She's really excited about it."

"Oh, it's my pleasure. Holly's really talented and very sweet. And I can tell she looks up to you." She cleared her throat, and it was evident she was struggling to get the words out. "Listen, Erik, I . . . I had such a great time with you. I think you're awesome, gorgeous, and smart. I really hope we can still be friends."

I took her hand and felt her fingers tremble in mine. I couldn't remember ever having these strong feelings for a girl who I barely knew. "I don't want to be your friend."

She nodded and gulped. "I get it."

I squeezed her thigh under the table. "No, Aria, you don't. That's not what I meant. I like you. You're beautiful and smart and honest . . . and you intrigue me. I love that you say what's on your mind and not what you think I want to hear. You challenge me. I've always wanted to date someone who is as dedicated to a goal as I am dedicated to being a SEAL."

"Well, I definitely share your drive. And your goals."

What did she mean by that? I didn't ask. "Many women want to have sex with a SEAL, but most women won't even consider being in a relationship with one. I'm gone all the time. We may only have a month together, but honestly, that's more time than I ever have had to get to know someone."

She gulped. I could tell she had something on her mind.

"Well, let's just have fun while we can. Who knows what the future holds."

I stroked my thumb back and forth over her knuckles. "Where are you going when you leave here?"

"Back east. Just some more training."

Her vagueness annoyed me. "Are you trying to compete for another Olympics?"

"Not sure. I'm going to see how this training goes."

"Well after this deployment, I may be around in San Diego for a while. Non-deployable."

Her brows raised. "Really? Doing what?"

"Can't say. But there are many different positions in the Teams." I reached over and gave her a kiss. "I get off in an hour."

"In an hour? That's like ten a.m. I thought you SEALs worked so hard."

"Yeah. When we are in country, we mostly train."

"Okay. Text me when you get off."

She leaned into me, and I touched her face, planting a sensual kiss on her lips. I relished her sweet taste and the heat of our breaths mingling together. A long moment later, I reluctantly let her go. "See you later, Aria."

I started to walk back to base but couldn't help but glance back at her. She flashed a shy smile that did a funny thing to my insides.

I strode back to her. "Hey, do you want to come to work with me? I can show you around."

Her hands clapped together. "Are you sure?"

"Yeah. We always welcome Olympians. Though I have to

warn you—my commander might force you to give a speech on why 'it pays to be a winner.'"

"Ha. I'd love to. Let's race."

And with that, she ran off in front of me, making a hard left out of the hotel. I sprinted after her, and when I reached her, I grabbed her from behind and threw her down onto the sand. As we rolled on the beach, I pinned her under me and kissed my girl.

14

ARIA

E rik walked me on base and proudly introduced me to his friends. I couldn't believe this place. There were gorgeous men everywhere I looked, but I was in the arms of the hottest one of them all.

I had always imagined these badass Navy SEALs to be complete assholes. So tough, so hard. But ever since I'd met Erik, I kept being shocked at how sweet he was. Masculine no doubt, but he seemed to care about everyone around him. His mother, his sister, and me. And now he wanted to date me.

I had to tell him the truth.

"Lieutenant Commander Lawson, this is Aria Clements. You two have a lot in common. She's an Olympic athlete. Lawson over here used to be a professional football player."

"Nice to meet you, Aria. You can call me Kyle."

I shook Kyle's hand and began to gush. "I read about you! You gave up your multi-million dollar contract to become a SEAL. Didn't you save your wife from terrorists?"

His brow cocked. "I did. It wasn't a big deal. Just another day on the job. The damn media outed me when we had our wedding. But it's cool. We've worked with some of the Olympians who train down here in Chula Vista. Would you like to run our obstacle course? Erik can show you how it's done."

Oh my God! Yes. I'd dreamed of having a crack at the world-famous obstacle course. I needed to remain cool. "I'd love to."

Erik grabbed my hand. "I'll make you a deal. I'll show you how to do the "O" course if we go on a bike ride later today."

Worry coiled through my body. Getting a shot at the "O" course was the opportunity of the lifetime. It would give me an advantage that no one else had going into BUD/S next year. And I rationally knew that I had a bigger chance of getting injured on the course than I did getting injured on the bike. Still, it was a mental barrier.

One I needed to break.

"Ok, deal."

He grinned. "Let's go, champ."

Champ. A flush rose to my cheeks. He had called me that when he was going down on me. I couldn't wait to be intimate with him again.

We walked over to the daunting tower and saw a few SEALs climbing the ropes.

Erik pulled me into his arms and kissed me. "You finish the "O" course now; I'll give you an "O" later."

"But I'm just a girl!" I teased. "I couldn't *possibly* complete it. It's made for you big, muscular men. I don't have the strength or the endurance."

He tickled me. "Smartass. I'll test your endurance later. Let me show you how it's done."

He ran in front of me, leaving me in the dust. First, he climbed on the parallel bars and pushed himself to the other end. Then he ran through the tires before climbing over a low wall. God, he was so ridiculously hot. When he had run over the tires, he had clasped his hands behind his neck, and I was mesmerized by his muscular forearms, his abs, and his massive thighs. Erik made everything look so effortless, but I knew how hard it all was. He ran over to an even taller wall, climbed the rope, and jumped off that one as well. I continued to watch, transfixed, as he low-crawled under some barbed wire before scaling the cargo net and running over some logs. Then he effortlessly jumped on the infamous Dirty Name obstacle.

I knew from studying that it had two hurdles—one at five feet and one at ten with four feet in between. He jumped up, belly flopped on the first hurdle, rose to his feet, and belly flopped on the second before jumping off. He ran over a few more logs, weaved in and out of this wood contraption before climbing another rope and walking on a horizontal rope that made a bridge, looking like a tightrope walker. Erik ran over a few more logs, then up a huge series of wooden platforms before he slid down the rope head first—the slide for life. Another rope swing led him to some monkey bars, up to a flat wall, over some vaults, and then finally he returned to me.

My entire body tingled and heat pooled between my legs. I was so turned on by his strength.

Before I could speak, he handed me a helmet.

"Your turn, champ."

I strapped the helmet on my head, and my heart palpitated. "Let's do it."

I ran through the first few obstacles without a hitch. Crawling under the sharp barbed wire caused my insides to shake, but I kept my body low and made it out. I spat the grainy sand out of my mouth and ran toward the next obstacle. My forearms burned as I climbed yet another rope.

"That's it, champ. You're doing amazing." His praise invigorated me. I wanted to make him proud of me.

The cargo net was also a challenge, making sure to get a firm footing on the ropes. I'd read about one man who had become a paraplegic when his foot got caught in the netting. I pushed my fear aside, and I climbed to the top and backed down the other side.

But then I came face to face with Dirty Name.

Erik was right by my side. "Babe. This one is called Dirty Name. You got this. Just jump up on the first log and then throw yourself over the first hurdle. Aim for your waist."

Okay. That didn't sound too hard.

Taking a deep breath, I gathered all my strength and jumped up and flew onto the hurdle. But instead of landing on my stomach, I crashed down right on my breasts and fell to the ground.

Dammit.

Erik ran over to me. "You okay?"

"Yup. Never better."

"Most people can't get through that obstacle. It counts for most of our drops during hell week."

"Let me try again," I insisted.

"Have at it."

I ran back a few feet and had a running start. Again, I jumped on the first log and trying to hoist my body over the first hurdle. But this time, I jumped, and the hurdle hit above my chest, knocking my wind out of me. Dammit.

"Don't worry about it. Just go to the next obstacle."

"No. I want to try again."

He narrowed his eyes at me. "Aria, come on. It took me weeks to master this. Let's just move on."

But I couldn't move on. The bitter taste of failure hung heavy on my tongue. "Please, just one more time."

He nodded, and I ran again. This time I landed smack on my ribs. I swear I heard a crack, but it could also have been my audible shame.

"Babe. You're incredible. Come on. Let me gather my stuff, and we can get out of here."

"Can I finish the rest of the course?"

"Sure."

Luckily, the rest of the course seemed easier. I had no problem with the logs. I gasped when I looked down at the ground so far away from me as I tiptoed across the rope. The slide of life was intimidating as it seemed like I was gliding head first into the Pacific Ocean, but I just focused on my balance. I had no problem on the monkey bars or up to the flat wall or vaults. When I ran to the finish line, Erik lifted me into his arms and kissed me.

"Aria, you take my breath away. I can't believe you just did that. You should be so proud of yourself."

But I didn't feel proud. I felt shame, humiliation, defeat. I had to master Dirty Name. I could hear the voice of my mom ring in my head. "You'll never be good enough."

I looked at Erik, his face beaming with pride. I hated myself. Here I had this amazing supportive man, and I was deceiving him. I was really starting to care about him, but I couldn't imagine how hurt he would be when he found out I was training to be a SEAL. He would think that I was dishonest and deceptive when that wasn't true. Had he told me that he supported female SEALs, then I would've been honest with him.

I needed to come clean to him and tell him the truth. I just prayed that he would still look at me the way he was looking at me now.

15

ERIK

I changed out of my uniform and into my street clothes. Man, Aria killed it on the "O" course, even if she hadn't conquered Dirty Name. Ever since our fight about women in combat, I had given serious thought to my opinions on the matter. I had always contended that a woman could never complete BUD/S. But what about a woman like Aria? A champion, an athlete, an overachiever. Bottom line, my opinion had been challenged but not changed. Even if a woman could graduate from SEAL training, which I still doubted was possible unless we lowered our standards, I still believed in my soul that there was no place for women on the Teams.

I planted a kiss on her head. "Let's go rent you a bike."

She winced. "I know I promised. And I will for sure but can we do it next weekend?"

"Why? Are you too tired from the "O" course?" I teased.

She shook her head. "No. That's not it."

I paused to examine her beautiful face. "Then what is it?"

Her chest caved. "You're going to think I'm a weirdo if I tell you."

"Spill it. Did you crash on a bike once?"

"No." She lowered her voice to a whisper. "I don't know how."

Wait, what? "You're kidding me. You're an Olympian. You just owned the Naval Special Warfare "O" course, a course that has made grown men cry, and you are telling me you have never ridden a bicycle?"

"I know. I know. It's ridiculous. There is this long embarrassing story behind it. . ."

I took her hands. "I'm all ears, champ. Lay it on me."

Her face turned into a grimace, and she swallowed. "My mom never bought me a bike. You see, I grew up in Marin on the top of this winding hill in Corte Madera, and she was afraid I'd get injured and then not be able to swim. But then when I was accepted to Stanford, everyone biked to class, and I wanted to fit in, ya know?"

"Yeah... go on."

She cleared her throat. "So, I bought a brand-new bike, figuring I was a champion swimmer so how hard could it be to learn how to ride a bike. But, then when I went to ride one day, I ... panicked. Like what if my mom was right? What if I fell and twisted my ankle? I mean, I had been training for the Olympics my entire life. One injury like that could destroy everything, my entire life's work. So yeah, I never learned. Now, it's a thing."

"Wow." I studied this fearless woman in front of me. A woman who embraced challenges. But a woman who didn't seem to be able to relax and enjoy life. "Thanks for telling me. Now let's go to the bike shop."

She bit her lip. "Wait, why? I just told you I've never ridden a bike."

"Right. So, it's time for you to learn."

She shook her head and grabbed my arm, her eyes wide and pleading. "No, seriously. Now's just not the right time. One day I'll learn. Maybe when I have kids. But now, it would be too risky."

I lifted her chin up with my thumb and stared into her eyes. "How would it be risky? The next Olympics aren't for another three years. You told me you don't know what you're doing next. Now's a perfect time. Live a little, baby. It's just a bike, not a motorcycle. My buddy's five-year-old son can ride without training wheels. You will be fine."

Her eyes turned a darker shade of green, and she fired a glance at me. "I said no. Just drop it, okay?"

"Fine," I bit out.

She touched my shoulder. "Sorry, I didn't mean to snap."

"Don't worry about it." Why did her reluctance to ride a bike bother me so much? I paused for a minute to figure out my thoughts. It wasn't that she wouldn't try something new with me; it was that I was certain she was holding back a huge part of her life from me. Like she had made a decision and already knew exactly what she planned for the future, yet she refused to tell me. What could it be? Had she accepted a job somewhere far away? Joined the circus? I didn't have a clue and refused to speculate anymore.

But I was determined to get answers.

We walked down the beach, and she leaned up to me. "I have a better idea anyway."

"What?"

Her hand reached around me, and she squeezed my bicep. "Let's go back to my place. I've missed you."

Fuck yeah. I pulled her body into mine and my cock

pressed against her thigh. "You're right. That is a better idea."

She laughed, and I kissed her in front of the Del, the waves crashing on the shore nearby. She escaped my embrace and jogged down the beach, and I chased her. I couldn't wait to get her alone.

16

ARIA

My stomach fluttered from the anticipation of being with Erik again.

And this man. Oh my god. The things he did to me. I was so turned on watching him slay the "O" course. And then he fulfilled my dream by allowing me to try it.

But the best part of all wasn't watching him or even him letting me have a crack at it. The best part by far was the way he made me feel when I completed some of the obstacles. I'd been trained by top coaches who had believed that the only way to get someone to succeed was to berate them.

"Aria, you are slow like turtle and have arms like noodle," my coach Olga used to yell at me. "Your feet look like duck. Are you duck? Quack Quack."

It was almost comical to think back on it now. But at the time, those words destroyed my soul.

But Erik calling me champ, believing in me, cheering me on . . . the look on his face when I finished the slide of life, that type of encouragement made me want to do better, make him proud.

If only I could have his support and aid going through BUD/S, then without a doubt I would make it.

I ran up the street where my cottage was and after opening the gate, and my front door, Erik followed me eagerly inside.

I let Flounder out into the yard, and before I even stepped foot back into my place, Erik pinned me to the wall.

I writhed under his body, his big, strong chest pressing against mine. He kissed down my neck, but I escaped from his grip. My hands explored his arms, tracing his muscles before I lifted his shirt off. We'd fucked in the ocean, and he had pleasured me back at his place.

But now it was my turn to take control.

I undid his belt with a single motion, and his shorts dropped to the floor.

"Yeah, baby. Suck my cock."

Yes, sir. I should salute. Well, he was an officer. My hands squeezed his firm ass, and I pulled down his black boxer briefs. His cock was gorgeous. Hard, long, thick. I couldn't wait to suck him off.

I grasped his balls in my hand and kissed around the base, inhaling his masculine, virile scent. Maybe he had been right about not having females on the Teams. This man was so hot that I had to admit I'd be jealous if I was his wife back home and he deployed with a woman. But I focused my thoughts back on my current mission. To give him the best blowjob he had ever had.

"Stop teasing me, babe."

I licked down his length and spat on my hand before I grasped him. A few more kisses on the head before I took him in my mouth. He exhaled and ran his fingers through my hair.

"That's it, baby. You like my cock in your mouth?"

I fucking love it. My mouth bobbed up and down, taking him as deep as I could while using my hand to also please him. I created a seal with my lips, his head pressing on the back of my throat.

I loved submitting to him, pleasing this sexy man. The only man who I felt had ever seen the real me. Not the champion, but the timid, insecure woman who was afraid to express her needs.

My current need was him.

I could feel a shift. He began to take control back from me, pulling my head into him, fucking my mouth. It felt dirty, illicit. I couldn't get enough of his cock.

"Damn. Your mouth is so hot."

I dug my nails into his ass as he thrust his cock deeper into my mouth.

"I'm going to come, baby."

I can't wait. He tried to pull away, but I wouldn't let him. I sucked him so hard, so deep, craving to taste him. He grunted and filled my mouth with his hot cum, and I lapped up every bit and then swallowed.

"Fuck yeah, Aria. Damn. You deserve a gold medal for that performance."

I wiped my mouth. "You haven't seen anything yet. That was just preliminaries."

He laughed, pulled up his boxer briefs and then embraced me. "I'm crazy about you, do you know that?"

I felt it. I saw it in his eyes. But I was holding something back. I could never fall in love with this man or let him fall in love with me until I was honest with him.

I let Flounder back in the house. "Do you want to come

with me to Isa's house tomorrow? She and her husband are having a superhero costume party for their anniversary."

"Sure. I've met Grady once. Guy's a fucking badass. I'd be honored to get hammered with him." He cocked his brow. "Who are we going as?"

I gave him a playful grin. "Aquaman and Wonder Woman. We can work on our costumes tomorrow."

He laughed and gave me a wink. "Kickass, but I already have a costume. Aquaman is my favorite superhero. You know, the first time Orin and Diana met before they became Aquaman and Wonder Woman, Triton attempted to take her away before Orin saved her. They kissed passionately before parting ways."

I pinched him. "I detect a hint of geekiness. Don't get me wrong . . . it's sexy. Let me guess; you go to Comic Con every year."

"Damn straight. We should go together next month and cosplay."

My chest tightened, knowing I would be in Officer Candidate School. "That would be fun. Maybe next year."

He wrinkled his brow at me. I quickly changed the subject.

"Anyway, the party is at seven. You can just meet me here at six."

He sat on my sofa and grabbed the remote control. "Better yet, I'll just spend the weekend with you. I'll stop by my place later and pick up some stuff."

A lump grew in my throat. I had wanted to spend the rest of the day training. But maybe I could make some adjustments. I had already done the "O" course today.

And for the first time in my life, I had a glimpse of what it would be like to be in a real relationship. Could I ever be happy living outside of the limelight? Maybe I could love and support someone else's dreams instead of selfishly focusing on my own.

Or better yet, maybe we could lift each other up.

"Sounds good. You hungry?"

"Starved. I can order a pizza."

"No, it's okay. I have some food." Pizza was a treat I rarely indulged in. Despite how much I craved the gooey cheesy and greasy pepperoni, eating it just made me feel guilty.

I walked over the fridge and stared at the contents. Watermelon, grilled chicken, brown rice, eggs, and bell peppers. I was even depriving my refrigerator of having some fun.

"Actually, yeah, a pizza sounds good."

He grabbed his phone. "On it, babe."

I glanced back at him. This sex god was sitting on my sofa petting my dog. Today had already been such an incredible day. Erik had shown up at my class, forgave me for storming out of his place, and had let me run the "O" course.

I vowed to embrace the rest of the time I had left with him. Really explore having a relationship.

But first, I had to tell him the truth.

17

ERIK

I pulled on the leather pants that I'd purchased last year for Halloween and clutched my massive trident, though the long metal spear couldn't ever replace my real trident that had been pounded into my flesh upon my BUD/S graduation. Standing there with my class, looking at my family in the audience, my father's face beaming with pride, without question had been the best day of my life.

"Babe, let's go. I don't want to be late."

Aria emerged from the bathroom door, and one look at her caused my heart to beat strong in my chest. Stunning, simply stunning. She wore thigh high red and gold boots, a short blue skirt over black boy shorts, a red bustier, and a long black wig.

"Damn, woman. I'm going to be fighting off men at this party."

She laughed and then whipped her gold lasso at me.

I grabbed the lasso and wrapped it around her. "We can use this later tonight."

"Sounds like a plan."

My hand clutched her ass, and I kissed her. My hand traced over the metallic rope. The truth lasso. If only it actually worked. Then I would be able to force her to be honest with me. "Let's go, babe."

We left her place and got into my car. I drove over the bridge and headed toward Grady and Isa's place. I was looking forward to talking to Grady alone, find out what really happened to him in Iraq, off the record. I knew too well how the media embellished war stories. Grady was no doubt a hero, but I wanted to hear his account in his own words.

I was also curious to see Aria in a casual party setting. Would she let loose? Get drunk? Have a good time? I worked my ass off, but I also knew how to chill out.

Aria gripped my thigh. "So, I know you can't tell me details of your job. But, in general, what are deployments like? Where do you go?"

I appreciated her interest in my job. Most girls I'd dated didn't care at all about it, even if they had pretended that they thought it was cool that I was a SEAL.

"Afghanistan, Somalia, Syria. We go everywhere, but different Teams have different regions."

"What's your exact job?"

"Well, I'm an officer, but a junior one. Kyle is my superior officer. But SEALs are all operational, officers and enlisted. I plan the missions, interpret Intel. I was an Economics major at Annapolis."

Her eyes widened. "Wow. That's so cool. I considered majoring in comparative literature, but I ended up declaring HumBio."

"What's that?"

She blushed. "Oh. Sorry. Stanford lingo. Human Biology— the relationship between biology and social science. It's really cool. I was pre-med also."

"Really? So, are you going to apply for med school? UCSD has a great one. And they are the Tritons."

She averted her eyes. "Maybe. I'm not sure."

There she went again . . . being evasive. "You aren't sure about what? I'm finding it hard to believe you don't have every minute of your life mapped out."

"Oh. Um . . ." She removed her hand from my thigh and looked out the window. "I already told you that I'm going to train back east after this summer. Then I'll figure out what I'm doing."

I tapped my fingers on the steering wheel. Why was this bothering me so much? I really liked this girl but I had only known her for two weeks so why did I care that she wasn't opening up to me?

We arrived at Grady and Isa's complex near San Diego State University. Isa buzzed us in, and we walked into their apartment. It definitely contrasted from my bachelor pad. Though the furniture was black, there were framed pictures, fresh cut flowers, and a bunch of those throw pillows on the sofa.

A few girls dressed as sexy superheroes and villains were talking to Isa, and there were a bunch of dudes who looked like jarheads milling around, but I didn't recognize any of them.

Isa greeted us dressed as Black Panther. "Hey, guys! Oh my god, you both look awesome."

Aria hugged her. "Thanks. So do you. Though with my red hair and your black hair we should probably switch superheroes."

Isa laughed. "I know, right? Yeah, it's a joke. You see I met Grady at a frat party. He was dressed as Hulk, and I was Black Panther. We went to the same party a month ago as

Harley Quinn and the Joker but it wasn't the same so we are back to being the Hulk and Black Panther. So we decided to hold an anniversary party and invite our friends. I can't believe it's been over a year since we met. If you had told me last year I'd be married, I wouldn't have believed you. Anyway, let me take you to meet my friends." Isa led Aria out to the patio.

Grady walked over to me. He dressed as Hulk but wasn't wearing a mask. A lump grew in my throat when he came into focus. I'd met him before, but every time I saw his face, I was reminded of the risks I took when I deployed. Grady was ripped and masculine, but half of his face was mangled and horribly scarred. I forced myself not to stare at his glass eye or his misshapen ear.

Grady shook my hand. "Hey man, thanks for coming."

"Anytime, bro. It's an honor to hang out with you."

I stared at his beautiful wife outside with Aria, noting how she looked at him so lovingly, as if he was the most hand-some man in the world. I wondered what it would be like to find a woman who loved me the way Isa loved Grady. Could Aria be that woman? I had my doubts, especially since she refused to talk about any future with me nor even clue me into her plans for the next year.

"Can I get you a beer?"

"Yeah. That would be great."

Grady went to the fridge and grabbed two bottles of local craft lemon shandies. He squeezed a lemon wedge through the neck and handed me one.

I knocked his bottle with mine. "Cheers man."

"Cheers."

He took a swig, and I did as well. It tasted refreshing—like a glass of summer.

"How you've been?" I asked.

"Good, dude. Trying to get through school but I have another surgery next month. I'm doing some work with wounded warriors, but the pay sucks," he grimaced. "Not sure how much longer I can afford to do it. I still get offers to write a memoir, but I'm not into it. And I'm asked all the time to do speaking engagements . . . but I'd probably just have panic attacks, so I don't know."

My eyes scanned his place. It was nice and modern, but small. This badass was a medal of honor recipient. He'd jumped on a bomb to save his friends' lives. Rage filled me when I thought about the celebrities who lived in mansions while Grady was struggling to make ends meet, medically retired from the military, unable to serve the country he loved. The entire situation pissed me the fuck off.

"That sucks, man. I respect the hell out of you. And I agree with you about not wanting to write a book. Most of the Team guys I knew who wrote them completely regretted it."

"Yeah. It would all be some fake war propaganda. There isn't that much to say. What do they want to write about? My fucked-up childhood? Basically, a grenade was thrown into the building I was clearing, and I jumped on it. End of story. The rest would just be a pity fest."

Now I liked this guy even more. Even some of the SEALs I met bragged about our missions. Grady was so humble. "Don't downplay it, dude. You're a beast."

"Thanks. I appreciate that." His gaze trailed off toward his wife, who was chatting with Aria, and his expression softened. "I'll tell you, man; I wouldn't still be here if I hadn't met Isa. Before she came in my life, I had some dark times. I'd spent months wishing the bomb had killed me. She really saved me."

Fuck. His words chilled me. I'd lost some of my own buddies to suicide. I patted his shoulder. "Well, I'm glad you found her. I've talked to her a few times at the pool, and she's great. And she's crazy about you."

"Well, it's mutual. I still can't believe how lucky I am. Hey, do you guys have that new Glock 19? I've been dying to shoot it."

"Hell yeah. It's awesome. I still love my Sig, but the Glock is smaller. Do you want to come shoot on our range? I'd be honored to take you anytime."

The half of his face that wasn't scarred lifted and he smiled. "You mean it, man? The civilian ranges suck."

"Yup, anytime." I took out my phone, and we exchanged numbers.

"I'll take you up on that."

I placed my hand on his shoulder. "One more thing. I know you have Isa, but if you ever need to talk to someone who has been through war, call me. I mean it. I know you have your buddies, but I'm here for you."

He swallowed. "Thanks, man. I appreciate it. I'm going to go feed everyone." He brought a platter of burgers out to the grill.

Aria came back inside. "How long do you want to stay?"

I gave her a blank look. "What? We just got here?"

Her shoulders were slumped, and she pulled her hair. "I know. Isa is super nice, but I don't know anyone else here. I just am not much of a party girl."

"That's the point of a party, babe. You get to know other people. Do you want a drink?"

She shook her head. "No, I missed my workout today so I shouldn't."

I took both of her hands in mine and gazed down at her. "Aria, you are in perfect shape. Just relax a bit."

"I can't. I came to Coronado to train, and I've been spending time with you, so I'm behind."

"Behind on what? What are you training for exactly?"

She pulled her hair and looked away from me. "Nothing. You're right." She looked around the kitchen, extricated herself from my grip, and poured herself a rum and coke in a red solo cup. "Hey. I wanted to tell you something."

"What's up?"

"I like that you keep trying to push me out of my comfort zone."

"I just want you to live a little, sweetheart. I spent six months of my life in BUD/S training. I was so focused. Didn't want to let my dad down. But he died right after I graduated. He invited me to a Padres game once, and I didn't go because I was training. I regret not taking the time to have fun."

She gave me a sympathetic nod and stroked my forearm. "Wow. I'm sure he understood."

"Yeah. Well, I can't go back in time. I'd been so focused on school, my career. I want to make my personal life a priority."

A shadow crossed her lovely face. "I don't even know what that means. I've never even had a boyfriend."

My heart hammered in my chest, and a wave of possessiveness surged through me. "Well, you have one now."

She opened her mouth and then closed it quickly, her gaze darting between my eyes and the floor. "I like you, Erik. I really do…more than you can possibly know. But I'm leaving. I just don't see how this can work out."

"Doesn't matter that you are leaving. Any relationship I'm in is long distance. You could be in another country, and it wouldn't make a difference. I'll be halfway around the world next month."

She took a step back from me. "Look, I really care about you. It's just—"

"Just what? What are you so afraid of, baby? We're perfect for each other."

"But…how can you even *say* that? You don't even know me!"

I pulled her into my arms and held her close, forcing her to look at me. "You're drop dead gorgeous. But it's so much more than that. We're both over achievers . . . and you inspire me. I'll never be lazy with you. And I can teach you to have some fun, too. I'm a SEAL officer, and I want a strong woman like you beside me. Give me a chance."

Tears welled in her eyes. "I'm sorry, Erik...my life is just so complicated right now that I can't even think about anything long-term. Can't we just enjoy our time together until I leave and then figure things out from there?"

"Fine." I pounded my beer and left her in the kitchen. I wasn't delusional. I knew she was attracted to me. I could see the way she looked at me, feel the way she touched me. If any part of me thought that she wasn't interested in me, I'd back off. But that wasn't it. Something was holding her back, and I didn't have a clue what it was.

But I was a SEAL—and SEALs never quit.

I'd just have to break down her walls and make her mine.

18

ARIA

We kept our distance for the rest of the party until I finally convinced him to leave. I hated myself right now. What on earth was I doing? I had this amazing guy, the type of man that my mom had repeatedly told me would never be interested in me, and I was pushing him away. He was insanely hot, incredible in bed, a Navy SEAL, sweet to his family, educated, and supportive. I'd be an idiot not to try to make a go of it with this man.

Okay. Tonight. I was going to tell him *tonight*.

If he liked me as much as he claimed, it wouldn't change his feelings toward me. He could help train me and be there for me through BUD/S.

If we are meant to be, it will all work out. If he has a problem with it, I'll be devastated, but at least it won't be a shock. I already know his views on the matter. I'm proceeding at my own risk.

There was no certainty about relationships. My mom had never been in a stable one, so I didn't even have a role model to aspire toward. I could only rely on myself, and as much as I cared about Erik, I couldn't let anything stand in the way of me achieving my goals.

He drove back to my place in silence. When we arrived, I invited him in, and to my relief he accepted. I let Flounder out and then sat on the porch, staring up at the stars.

My phone buzzed. Eight missed calls from my mom. I could not deal with her right now.

When Flounder was done taking care of business, we went back inside my place. Erik was sitting on the sofa with a stone hard expression on his face. Was he still mad at me? I couldn't tell what he was thinking. Or feeling. And it killed me.

I sat next to him, my heart pounding in my chest, and nearly wept with relief when he put his arm around me.

"I'm sorry. I—"

He pressed a finger to my lips. "Don't. It's fine, baby."

"No. I owe you an explanation."

"Aria, you don't owe anyone anything. Just do whatever you got to do in your life. I'll be here when you're done."

I blinked back tears. What had I done to deserve his blind loyalty? I knew the answer to that. Nothing. Why did he even like me? I could never be good enough for an incredible guy like him. "You mean that?"

"I do. I'll be around until you leave, and then I deploy. It's not like I'll be dating when I'm in Iraq. You know, since women still aren't on the Teams."

I punched his arm. "Smart ass."

"No seriously. Go and do whatever it is that is next in your life. We can stay in touch while I'm gone. And we can see where we're at when I return."

My body flushed with warmth. I straddled him and looked into his eyes.

Say it, dammit. Tell him the truth.

But no words came out of my mouth. He reached behind my neck and undid my bustier as easy as if he was picking a lock. My breasts bounced free, and the cool air hardened my nipples.

He pulled my wig off, and I shook my hair free as it cascaded over my breasts.

"Aria," he rasped as he planted kisses on my neck. "You're so sexy."

I squeezed the muscles in his arms, slowly tracing the intricate ink from his tattoos. What were the stories behind his body art? Tribal patterns were interwoven with some script. There was so much about this man that I had yet to discover. But all I knew was I needed to get lost in him, feel his strong arms encircling my body. For so long I had been so independent, relying on no one but myself. But for as long as I was with him, I would depend on him.

I flipped back my hair as he buried his face into my chest. The warmth of his tongue excited me, and I gasped when he sucked on my left nipple as his hand worked on my right one. My own hands became addicted to his body, kneading his muscles, stroking his back, never wanting to let go.

I let out a moan when his mouth switched to my other nipple. My enthusiastic response invigorated him. He grasped my hair in his fist, kissed me aggressively, his tongue probing my mouth.

He pulled my panties down over my legs, leaving my boots on. I hiked up my skirt and wrapped my legs around his waist, desperate to feel his hard cock.

"That's it, baby. Rub your pussy all over me. I'm going to get you off before I fuck you. I want to watch you come."

He grasped my hips, situating me closer, and began to rock me back and forth.

His mouth went back to work on my nipple, and his other hand massaged my breast.

"Oh my god, baby. That feels so incredible."

I swiveled my hips around as I grasped his thighs. I was so close to coming, but I wanted to hold on to this edge of ecstasy.

He spread my legs wide and pulled me into him and rubbed me over his hard cock. "Come for me now, champ."

"Oh! Yes! Yes!" My breath hitched, and I crashed into paradise, riding him and savoring every last second of my orgasm.

He cradled me in his arms as I relaxed in his embrace. Enjoying the perfect beauty of the moment.

He leaped up and stripped off his leather pants. As he stood stark naked in front of me, I marveled at how ridiculously hot this man was. He had a better physique than any Olympian I'd ever met, and the hair on his chest made him look so masculine, so virile. I'd found other men sexy, but I had never felt an insatiable hunger for anyone else as I had for Erik.

With one arm, he flipped me around, and his hand slid

down my belly and landed in between my thighs. His finger parted my lips as he pressed it inside me and then slowly removed it. He angled my ass up, gripped my waist, as the tip of his cock pushed into me. He was so hard, and I was so wet, the perfect combination of pressure and ecstasy sent me soaring again.

He filled me up as he went deeper and deeper, fucking me so hard I was panting as if I had just run four miles.

"You have the perfect ass, baby." He spanked me, and I moaned.

"Ooh."

"You like that? You like it rough? Are you my dirty girl?"

"Yes!"

He pulled my hair as if it was in a ponytail and spanked me again.

The sting from his hand on my ass contrasted with the pure pleasure of his cock inside my body. My clit was throbbing, and I was desperate to come again, come with him. I could feel his pace quicken, his breath coming in hot spurts on my neck.

"Erik!" I screamed. My hands clutched the sofa as he pounded into my pussy again and again until there was no him and no me, just us as one, coming together.

He held me tight as I quivered and I wanted to stay in this moment forever.

But I knew that we could never return to this perfect time. Once I told him my truth, he would never feel the same about me as he did right now.

19

ERIK

I had a brutal week of training out at San Clemente Island. My Team was flown out of Coronado up the coast to spend some time blowing up buildings and practicing raids. We even trained on a full-scale replica of Osama Bin Laden's compound. Honestly, I had a blast and couldn't believe that I was lucky enough that this was actually my job. Most days, I felt like I was living in a video game. But even so, I missed Aria.

Reception sucked, and Wi Fi was nonexistent. I'd explained this to her before I'd left and she was cool with it. I was so grateful to meet a girl who understood my job—my last girlfriend would always get upset when I couldn't call, text, or email. Not that I had a choice—I was married to the Teams.

I flew back into Coronado on Sunday and called Aria. She

invited me over to her place, but first, I had some shopping to do.

I walked down Orange Ave and went to Holland's Bicycles. I spent around twenty minutes browsing different bikes before I chose an Electra Cruiser in Sea foam.

I paid for the bike and a helmet. The shop girl eyed me. "Wow. Nice bike. Must be a lucky lady."

I smiled. "She's not the lucky one; I am."

I left the store and walked the bike to Aria's place when my phone rang. It was that potential client.

"Hello, Mr. Johnson. How are you?"

"Fine, Erik. Just fine. The CFO will be in town next weekend. I want him to meet you. I was wondering if we could have dinner together next Friday."

I had to ask Aria to accompany me. "Of course, sir."

"Wonderful. I'll make reservations at Addison for 6:00."

I tried not to laugh. Addison was the same place my mom suggested I take Aria out for a first date. "Wonderful, sir. I'll be there. Do you mind if a bring a date?"

"No, Erik. Not at all. We will be bringing our wives. I'll see you next week."

"Thank you, sir. I'm looking forward to it."

I hung up the phone, excitement racing through my chest. Mr. Johnson was a huge potential client who ran a biotechnology firm. I'd met him at a fundraiser for the Naval SEAL Foundation. Snagging him could take TritonFix to the next level.

I'd ask Aria tonight.

I turned down her street and opened the gate to her yard. Flounder greeted me with a sloppy kiss, and I rubbed his ears. Aria emerged from the house, and her eyes immediately focused on the bike.

"Erik, you didn't."

I leaned the bike against the fence and went in for a kiss. She tasted even sweeter than I remembered. "I did."

"Did you buy it or rent it?"

"I bought it, champ. It's all yours." I attempted to read her face. She bit her lip, and her brow contorted. What was she so afraid of?

I gave her another kiss. "Come on. You don't trust me?"

"No. That's not it. I do." She exhaled. "Okay . . . I'll give it a try."

"Good girl." I kissed the tip of her nose and took her hand in mine. Yet something felt...off. Once again, I experienced the gut feeling that she was holding something back from me. Some grand plan that she didn't want me to know. That was fine on our first date, but now that we'd slept together, I needed more. I wanted to be with someone who was open and honest with me.

"Let's walk over to my place and get my bike. We can start the trail from there."

We strolled by the beach as the tourists whizzed by us in their bikes. I often wondered how many of them were aware that Navy SEALs trained less than a mile away from their vacation.

She touched my arm—her delicate fingers sending spikes of heat through me. "So, what did you do this week?"

"A bunch of training evolutions. There's like a full city built out there. It's like a special forces Disneyland."

"Wow. That's so cool. I'd love to visit the island one day. I've read so much about it."

I eyed her. "Well, you can't. The island is restricted to the military. Unless you are a biologist. We occasionally have environmentalists come out to examine our impact on the native ecosystem. There are a couple of endangered species there—the San Clemente loggerhead shrike and the island fox." Leaning down, I pressed a gentle kiss to her forehead. "The entire island is really breathtaking. I'll show you pictures."

We made small talk as we headed to the parking garage under my condo to grab my bike. Then we walked to the trail in front of the Del.

"Hop on, champ. You have perfect balance. I've seen you pop out of the water on one foot."

She bit her finger nails. "It's different in the water."

"Get on the bike. I got you, babe. You're fine."

She strapped on the helmet, climbed on the bike, clutched the handle bars, and put both feet on the ground instead of the pedals. Waddling like a duck, within a few minutes, she maintained an awkward glide.

"That's it."

She stopped and just glared at me. "This is ridiculous. Everyone is staring at me."

I looked around, and a few tourists were gawking, but maybe they recognized her. "Forget about them. Get back on the bike."

She exhaled and then gave me a dirty look when a boy of around six lapped by her. But she mounted the bike again and placed her feet on the pedals. Though a bit wobbly at first, she slowly began to ride.

I hopped on my own bike. "See, you're a natural. It's easy." I yelled, but by now she was in front of me.

We biked through the neighborhoods and cut into Star Park where we passed L. Frank Baum's former residence, a two-story yellow house. I stopped on the sidewalk and showed her the Wicked Witch peering out from the side of the home and the Wizard of Oz sign hanging above the front door.

Her face beamed at the sight. "I loved the Oz books when I was a little girl."

"Yeah. He wrote Wizard of Oz here and based the Emerald City off the Del."

"I didn't know that. That's so cool. Thanks for showing me this."

We got back on the bikes and continued down the path. Aria had no problems keeping up with me at all. We headed to the North Island Naval Base, and we stopped in Bayview Park for a break.

She dismounted her bike and took a swig from her water bottle. We sat on a bench in the shade. I put my arm around her, drawing her close, and we gazed at the beautiful San Diego skyline.

"I can't thank you enough for forcing me to overcome my fear. It's been this secret of mine for years. I feel free. That was so much fun."

I grinned down at her. "It's hard for me to believe you are

afraid of anything."

"My entire identity is wrapped up in being an Olympian, Erik. At being the best. I often feel like people only like me for my accomplishments."

I leaned over and gave her a kiss under a towering tree. "I don't like you because you are a champion. That drew me to you at first, but you are so much more than your title. You are a beautiful woman. And you are adventurous and sexy." I tilted my head, and she leaned in to meet my lips. This wasn't our first kiss, but this time everything felt different. More intimate. The kiss was slower, yet laced with longing. When her hand reached behind my neck, a tingle shot through my body. With that jolt came a realization.

She was beginning to trust me.

Her hand gripped my upper thigh, and my cock ached for her.

I wanted to fuck her right there on the bench. But a chill took over me. I had to ask her if she would accompany me to dinner with my client next week. When I'd met her, getting her to help me with my business had been a goal. But now, I was falling for her.

I hoped I wouldn't erase all the progress we had made together by asking her for a favor.

20

ARIA

My feet sliced through the air, my hair blew in the wind.

Free. I felt free.

He had been right. Riding a bicycle, exploring this amazing island that I hoped to call home filled my heart with joy. I was delighted. I almost never took any time for myself. Sure, I'd indulge in a nice dinner after I'd won a competition or occasionally take in a movie with my teammates, but I never would just take a full day off and relax.

It was so much more than learning to ride a bicycle—it was a new way of life. I imagined living here. Maybe one day I'd settle down, possibly with Erik. Having our kids ride their bikes on the trails and spend their days at the beach.

And in my fantasy, I was happy.

Then why did I feel like the other shoe was about to drop?

Shaking off my worries, I just focused on having fun. Everything would work out the way it was meant to. We bought ice cream cones near the ferry, and I smiled at the children playing in the sand.

Emboldened by my new-found joy, I decided to ask Erik whatever I wanted, without being afraid that I would sound too forward.

"Do you want to have kids?"

"Of course I do. No time soon though. I deploy so much that I want to be around so I can spend time with my family. My dad was so involved."

I placed my hand on his bicep. "Your sister told me about your father. I'm so sorry. That must've been rough."

He looked up at me, blinking rapidly. "Yeah, it was brutal. He was a great man. My role model. I just miss him." He turned to me. "What about you? I know nothing about your family."

I winced. This was my fault; I had walked into this line of questioning. I was still too afraid to tell him I'd joined the Navy, but I vowed to be truthful with the rest of my life.

"Not much to tell. My mom had me when she was really

young. She never told my father that she was pregnant. I never met him."

Erik's head flinched back slightly. "Does he know you exist?"

"No. He died."

"I'm sorry. How?"

"I've actually never told anyone this. I just usually say he died." I took a deep breath. Here it went. "But I want to tell you. He joined the military. Actually, he was a SEAL."

And there it was. My secret. My truth. A fact so painful that I forced myself not to think about it. My father had been a SEAL. He had been killed in a helicopter crash.

And I wanted to be a SEAL. To be closer to him. To make him proud. We shared the same DNA. If he could make it, then why couldn't I?

Erik's eyes bugged. "No way. For real? What was his name?"

"Matthew Presley." Saying his name out loud for the first time in forever made him seem real.

"Wow. I didn't know you were a Frog Princess. You clearly share his drive. No man can graduate from BUD/S without being dedicated."

I sighed. "I'd like to think he was. I feel closer to him than ever since I've been in Coronado. Like he must've been at this shore, maybe shared an ice cream cone here. Meeting you has been such a blessing. I want to believe he was like you."

He reached out and grasped my fingers. "Baby, if you want, I can look him up. I'm sure I can find someone who served with him. Being a SEAL is like being in the most exclusive fraternity in the world."

"Thanks, I appreciate that." I swallowed a lump in my throat. "Maybe someday but I'm not ready yet. My mom never talks about him. All I know is that they were high school sweethearts, he enlisted in the Navy, and then she found out she was pregnant. I guess he wrote her, but she never responded. By the time I started asking about him, he was dead. I've wanted to reach out to his family, but they don't even know I exist."

He pulled me into his arms and rested his forehead against mine. "You should. They'd be so proud of you. I'd be happy to go with you to meet them."

I felt as if my chest was expanding, taking in his warmth and love. I cupped his face with my hands. "You're such a great guy, Erik. No matter what happens with us, I want you to know how much you've touched me."

"I want to touch you now. Let's go, champ. I've missed you all week."

Maybe, he could truly be my happily ever after fairy tale prince.

As we kissed in the sand like two teenagers in love a thought filled my head. I tried to push it away, but it was a gut feeling that permeated my soul.

I was going to marry this guy.

The more I fixated on it, the more I started to believe it. I saw a path for us. He would understand my drive. He would accept me. We could be happy together.

Hell, I deserved to be happy.

And tonight, I was the happiest girl on this island.

21

ERIK

After making out in the sand, Aria and I went back to her place. She cooked a Thai eggplant basil stir fry for dinner. It was spicy and sweet, just like her.

"Come here, babe."

The need built up in me, consuming my mind. To kiss her, to taste her, to fuck her.

My mouth claimed hers, but this wasn't a sweet, romantic kiss like we had shared on the shore. This kiss was filled with lust and longing. If I had missed her so much after only being away from her for a week, how could I possibly deploy away from her for months?

I wouldn't, couldn't, think about that now. All I could think about was how impossibly hard I was and how anxious I was to take her.

I wanted her differently than I had wanted her before. I wanted to fuck her hard and rough. Would she get scared when the gentleman officer was replaced by a dirty Navy SEAL?

With one arm, I removed her shirt and quickly snapped off her bra. She took my lead and unzipped her shorts and pushed down her panties. She grinned as they fell to the floor. Then I lifted her up, and she wrapped her legs around me before I slammed her back into the wall.

I slid my finger into her tight pussy.

"I want you so fucking bad, Aria. Every night in San Clemente, I was counting down the seconds until I could fuck you again."

"Then do it, Erik. Fuck me."

I dropped my shorts and pressed the tip of my cock to her opening. She gasped as I slowly entered her. She was slick and wet and felt like heaven.

My mouth crushed against hers, furiously kissing her while I fucked her. She bit my lips, and I pinned her wrists to the wall. Harder, faster, deeper. She met my rhythm, and her breath came in gasps.

I released her wrists, and she wrapped her arms around my neck. I cradled her gorgeous ass with my hands, kneading her into me.

I couldn't stop fucking her. I pounded into her again and again. Dying for her release, for my own.

"Erik! Erik!"

Every time she screamed my name I fucked her harder, deeper. My mouth found her nipples and I sucked until her screams turned into moans. Her pussy clenched around my cock, catching and releasing. I didn't want to stop—I wanted to fuck her forever. I slammed into her with a final thrust, and she exploded around me as I joined her in pleasure.

I stood still and took a moment to capture this beautiful picture in my memory so I could return to it forever.

When our bodies finally separated, I gave her a kiss. "I'm crazy about you, baby. You know that?"

She nodded, and I swore I saw a sheen of tears in her eyes. "I feel the same."

Life was good.

But I needed to ask her something.

I took one more long glance at her naked body, and I finally forced myself to step away from Aria. Our sexual chemistry was off the charts. Definitely enough sparks and memories to get through the long nights I would have without her when I deployed.

I gave her another long, lingering kiss and then went into her bedroom to change into my pajama bottoms. She followed quickly after me and threw on panties and a tank top, and we both prepared for bed.

I'd never lived with a girl, and I wondered what it would be like to come home to Aria, build a life with her.

She climbed under the covers, and I joined her.

Nibbling her bottom lip, she stared over at me. "What are you thinking about? You have a pensive look on your face."

I took a deep breath. I felt closer to her than ever. Now was my chance to truly open up to her. Tell her not only what I was feeling, but about my business, too.

I pulled her onto my chest and stroked her hair. "Lots of stuff. I never told you about my startup, did I? TritonFix?"

Her eyes widened. "No. I didn't know you could have a company while in the Teams."

"You can actually, you just have to get approval from your command. They make sure you aren't giving away top-secret information or disparaging the Teams. Hell, this one guy, a great SEAL, was recently caught making porn with his wife and some other women. He's probably going to lose his retirement."

"Wow. That's crazy. So, what's your business?"

"I provide consulting to businesses. Basically, I teach entre- preneurs how to apply military leadership within their companies. We conduct team building activities, go over different methods to build support structures in their office, and teach effective communication strategies. Honestly, I love it."

She turned to face me. "That's awesome, babe! You're so ambitious . . . which I think is super sexy by the way. I can see why they would hire you. You were so great with me out on the "O" course. More encouraging than my own coaches."

Her words invigorated me. Now was the time to ask her to meet my client. "Thanks, sweetheart. That means a lot to me. You know, I think it's the type of business you would be great in. Clients would love to work with a Stanford grad Olympian. If you aren't busy next Friday, I'm taking a potential client to dinner. Would you like to join me?"

The second those words left my mouth, I wished I could retract them. In an instant, the expression on her face went from adoring to a suspicious.

Her voice lowered to almost a whisper. "Why? Why do you want me there?"

"Because I'm proud to be dating you. Because you are beautiful. Because we are a couple."

"We aren't a couple." She rolled away from me and pulled the covers over her chest. "This is why you asked me out, right? You wanted to use me."

"What? No. Of course not. I was attracted to you and impressed by your accomplishments." Yes, I had initially pursued her with that intention, but I genuinely liked her. I wanted a *future* with her for fuck's sake.

"Sure you were. This isn't my first rodeo. I've been used before."

"I'm not using you, Aria." Fuck. Why was she reacting like this? Was it that wrong to want her to go with me to meet a new client?

A few minutes of awkward silence passed, so I nudged her. "Hey, I'm sorry I asked you. I didn't think it would be a big deal. You don't have to go if you don't want to."

"I'm just tired. Good night, Erik."

She didn't even turn around to give me a good night kiss. I decided to let it go and try to get some sleep, but I was becoming increasingly frustrated with her moods. What was she holding back from me? She was blowing hot and cold, and it was driving me insane.

But I refused to give up. I couldn't shake the feeling that Aria was the one for me, even if she didn't see me as her man.

22

ARIA

I waited for Erik to fall asleep. After around ten minutes, I turned over in the bed and saw his chest rise and fall.

As quietly as possible, I extracted myself from the bed. I grabbed some clean clothes from the top of my hamper and snuck out of the bedroom into the living room.

I laced up my running shoes and leashed up Flounder. It didn't matter that it was midnight—I needed to get the hell out of here. I didn't care if Erik woke up while I was gone. He was a smart man—he could figure out why I was livid. Maybe he'd come looking for me. Better yet, maybe he would leave.

The cool ocean night air hit my face when I left my place. I grabbed Flounder's leash and ran on the beach toward the

SEAL base. Despite Flounder's old age, he could still keep up with me, and I loved watching his long hound ears flap in the moonlight.

Flounder. What was I going to do about Flounder?

My mom had already told me that she wouldn't watch him when I went to Officer Candidate School. "Take him to the pound," she had said. "He's had a good life."

Fuck her. Flounder was the only one in my life who had always been loyal to me.

That was more evident today to me than ever.

I had one friend from back home who had offered to take him while I was gone, but she didn't really like dogs, and I felt she had offered more out of guilt because my mom had threatened to dump him at the shelter than out of a desire to love my dog.

Erik was great with my dog. And before tonight, I had considered asking him, especially since I had planned to tell him the truth about my plans.

But after what he had just asked me to do, all plans were off.

I continued to run down the beach past the lights of the Del. But brighter beams beckoned me just beyond the hotel.

Glow lights. Oh my god! It was hell week! It was Sunday night. Hell Week always started on Sunday. This had to be a sign!

I ran to the edge of the base where I was still on civilian land and stood there gawking in awe. There were around twenty-five men in front of me, carrying swift boats over their heads as their instructors yelled at them.

In six months, I would be one of them.

My heart chilled, and it wasn't from the lack of sunlight. I had to process what had just happened with Erik.

TritonFix.

My mom had been right. He had been using me. No matter what he had said, I didn't believe him. From day one, he knew who I was; he had targeted me. I knew a man as hot as he was could never be interested in me. I was an asset. Great on paper. "Hey guys, my girlfriend is an Olympic Gold Medalist. Let me tell you about my business and how I can help you achieve my goals. That will be ten thousand dollars."

Damn him. I refused to let him use me. My heart was crushed—how stupid I was for possibly believing he didn't have an ulterior motive for dating me. I shut my emotions down. I would kick him out of my place the second I returned tonight.

My eyes returned to the men in the water, their oars battling through the surf as their boats flipped over. Their sadistic instructors laughed at them as these poor candidates clung to their dreams.

A few instructors glanced my way. I didn't know if they had seen me with Erik, but none of them dared to approach me. Which was fine by me—at least they weren't shooing me away.

One of the boats came into shore. The men dropped into the sand and rolled around, getting wet and sandy.

And then I saw it. One man ran to his instructor. The instructor led him over to the bell, and he rang it three times.

A lump grew in my throat. That man had just quit. All his hard work washed away like an abandoned sand castle.

The rest of the men were now all out of the water. The instructors lined them up and ran them toward the back of the base.

Toward the "O" course.

I grabbed Flounder's leash and ran up the beach, past the Del, in front of Erik's condo building and toward the other side of the base. Though I had no ID card, I could see the "O" course from the road that ran along the Silver Strand

Boulevard. When I finally arrived, I peered through the wires on the fence as cars whizzed by, making sure I had a tight grip on Flounder's lead.

Sure enough, I had been right. Men were attacking the course. I waited for a few minutes, staring at Dirty Name. One by one, the men slayed it.

Until one man, a tall, skinny guy with black hair, fell. He picked himself up and tried again. And again. And again.

After a few more tries, an instructor walked over to him. The instructor placed his arm around the man's shoulders and walked him off the course.

And over to the bell.

That man was out.

My heart dropped. That man hadn't wanted to quit. I just knew it. He couldn't master one obstacle, a required obstacle during hell week. So he had been forced to ring the bell.

I didn't want to watch anymore.

I grabbed Flounder's leash and ran back toward my place.

What if I couldn't master Dirty Name? I needed every advantage I could get.

I had actually liked Erik. Up until tonight, I honestly thought we could have a future together if he accepted my career path. Initially, I had been so against dating him because I didn't want it to appear like I was using him.

But now, that had all changed.

He had charmed me with dinner and a girl power movie. I had slept with him. He had given me the opportunity to try Dirty Name. He had forced me to overcome my fear of riding a bike. I had fallen for him.

I had to turn off my feelings for him. Stop aching for him, making him my first thought in the morning and my last thought of the night. No more dreaming of a future together.

My worst fear had been realized. He liked me for what I had accomplished, not who I was.

I would never be good enough for a man like him.

I choked back a sob, realizing that he had been using me.

Well, two could play that game.

If he was going to use me, then I was going to use him.

I had one week left in San Diego. I'd go to dinner with his client. I'd pump Erik for information about BUD/S. And then I would demand to try the "O" course again.

After that. I was done with men. If I wanted to have sex, I'd have sex.

But I would never, ever listen to my heart again.

23

ERIK

The next morning, I had to leave early for work. I was surprised that when I woke up, Aria was already up. Her eyes were heavy, and her skin seemed puffy as if she had been up all night.

"Morning. I made you breakfast."

I stared at the plate she handed me. Scrambled eggs, bacon, and toast.

"Thanks. You didn't have to do this. But I appreciate it."

I sat at the table and ate as she stared at me, nursing a mug of coffee.

"I'll go to dinner with your client. I'm sorry I got upset last night. I was just caught off guard."

Her words made me happy, but her tone seemed hollow.

"Are you sure, babe? You don't have to."

"No, I want to. I leave next Sunday. We only have one week left together. I want to get in really good shape to train. Would you mind working out with me?"

That's my girl. "Not at all. I'd love to. Tell you what, I'll come by here when I get off, and we can go for a run and an ocean swim."

She blinked at me. "Sounds like a plan. Have a great day. I was up all night, so I'm going to get some rest." She gave me a kiss on the cheek and went into the bedroom and shut the door.

I looked at Flounder, who seemed to be as confused as I was.

"Women, buddy. I don't get them either."

I finished my breakfast and let myself out. As I ran to work, my stomach was in knots. I couldn't for the life of me figure Aria out. But from what I learned this weekend she had had a tough childhood. Maybe she just needed some patience and understanding. On the outside, she was this confident champion. But on the inside, she seemed conflicted. Vulnerable even. Sometimes I would see this wounded look in her pretty green eyes, and all I wanted to do was pull her close and kiss away her worries.

But she was making it so fucking hard because she kept those damn walls up.

Once I arrived on base, the first thing I did was go to our computer to look up her dad. I didn't think Aria was lying, but many men claim to be SEALs.

I typed in Matthew Presley.

A man with bright red hair and Aria's eyes popped up on my screen. Class #201. Wow, dammit. There was a brief bio listed. Everything she'd told me added up. Her dad had been part of SEAL Team 3 and had been killed in a helicopter crash.

There was no mention in the obituary of a daughter. Just like she had said—he hadn't even known she'd existed.

I missed my father so much it ached, but at least we had a great relationship while he was alive. I couldn't even imagine growing up without a father.

Guilt rushed through me. I had to be less hard on Aria, give her even more time. My parents had demonstrated for me the best example of a loving relationship. I needed to be patient with Aria.

I worked long hours for the rest of the week and spent my free time with Aria. Every day we worked out together, made dinner, made love, and went to bed. I couldn't put my finger on it, but I still felt like things were different between us than they had been before last week. But we only had this last week together, and I didn't want to put a damper on it, so I didn't bring it up.

Friday rolled around. I went to my place after work, took a shower, and dressed in my finest suit. I was used to my uniform, not evening wear. I shined my shoes, hopped in my sports car, and went to Aria's place.

She greeted me at the door wearing a sexy white dress and heels. I'd never seen her in heels and took a moment to admire her long, sexy legs.

"You look beautiful."

"Well, you look handsome, too."

Grabbing her hand, I escorted her to my car, and we hit the road. I drove over the bridge and headed north up the freeway. Once we exited the freeway, we drove through the guard gate of the resort. The Grand Del Mar couldn't be more different than Coronado's Del. While the Del was situated on one of the best beaches in the world, the Grand Del Mar was hidden in suburbia. Even so, the Grand Del Mar seemed more intimate, more romantic. It was no wonder that many celebrities and sports stars wed here.

I gave my car to the valet, took Aria's arm, and led her into Addison. The lobby was dim and rustic. High ceilings and arched windows led into a library and an ornate marble bar.

Aria whispered into my ear. "Wow, this place is so fancy. Reminds me of being in Europe."

"I've been around the world, but never to Europe." I flashed a grin her way. "I'd love to take you there someday, sweetheart."

"I'd . . . like that."

The hostess took my name and led us to the dining room. Mr. Johnson, a distinguished looking man with gray hair, a white beard, and sea blue eyes stood up to greet us. He introduced us to his wife, his business partner, Mr. Bradshaw, and his partner's wife. Then his eyes fell on Aria.

"Mr. Johnson, I'd like you to meet Aria Clements."

His kind eyes brightened when he saw her. "The Aria Clements? The Olympic Gold Medalist? What an honor to meet you."

He kissed her hand. "Thank you, sir. Thank you for inviting me. What a beautiful restaurant."

Mr. Johnson winked at me, and I smiled back. He was definitely impressed with my date.

We sat in a massive booth, and the waiter explained the menu.

The sommelier came by to go over the wine list, but we all decided to order the tasting menu with wine pairings.

I had prepared a long business spiel, but Mr. Johnson focused his attention on Aria.

"So, Aria. Do you live in San Diego?"

She took a sip of her champagne. "No, I still live up in Marin. I'm the celebrity Mermaid fitness instructor at the Del. This is, unfortunately, my last weekend here."

Mr. Johnson shot a glance at me. "Now Erik, you aren't going to let the mermaid swim away, are you?"

I placed my arm around her. "No, sir. I'm doing everything I can to make her stay."

Aria gave a forced smile, and I could feel her shift in her seat.

Mr. Johnson continued his line of questioning, clearly enamored with Aria. "Do you plan to compete in the next Olympics?"

"Honestly, I'm not sure. So many wonderful opportunities have been presented to me. The only thing I'm sure of is that I'm up for a new challenge."

I eyed her hard. What did she mean by that?

Our first course arrived—four Kumamoto oysters with

uni, caviar, a champagne foam with a hint of lemon. They tasted like pure ocean bliss.

Over the next six courses, we only briefly discussed business. But once the wine started flowing, the topics of conversation mostly fell to my thoughts on ISIS, North Korea, and the boastful SEAL who bragged about killing Bin Laden.

One whiskey cocktail, one glass of champagne, and six glasses of wine later, and I was definitely buzzed.

Mr. Bradshaw swirled his wine glass. "So Erik, what do you think of the rumors that the Navy SEALs are going to allow the first woman to try BUD/S?"

I almost choked on the glass of water I was sipping. Great. This was the last conversation I wanted to have in front of Aria. "Well, we haven't heard of anything in the pipeline yet." I looked over at Aria, her face turning red. "But, I'll be honest with you. No woman will make it through. And even if one could pass, she would ruin the cohesiveness of the Teams."

Aria stood up. "Pardon me; I need to go to the ladies' room." She hurried toward the back of the restaurant, and my stomach dropped. I had pissed her off again. I just hoped she would forgive me and come back. But this was a business dinner. They were interested in hiring me because

I was decisive and had convictions. I always said what I thought, even if it wasn't politically correct.

Mr. Johnson leaned over to me. "Son, you really impressed me tonight. For such a young man, you are very well spoken and intelligent. We find that our younger employees need someone that is more relatable. We would love to hire you to conduct a week-long training program for our employees."

Yes! I wanted to scream with elation as the warmth and pride radiated through my body. "Thank you, sir. I have some leave coming up next month. I'd be honored. This means a lot to me. I won't let you down."

"I know you won't. One more thing," he leaned in close, "don't let a woman like that get away. If you are as smart as I think you are, you'll marry her."

24

ARIA

Today was my final mermaid fitness class. Erik had insisted we stay at the hotel last night because we both had too much to drink. He drove me back over the bridge early for my class.

As I walked into the Del pool for the final time, Isa greeted me with a present.

I hugged her. "You shouldn't have."

"It's just something small. I'm so sad to see you go. Are you sure you can't do another month? All of our classes have been sold out because of you."

"I'm sure. I have another adventure lined up." I paused. "Hey, I noticed you guys don't have a dog. Is there any reason?"

She gave me a quizzical expression. "Actually, we were just

talking about getting one the other day. Grady wants an English Bulldog, so we've been looking at rescues. Why?"

I bit my lip. "I'm in a bind. I have to go away to train for a bit, but I'll be coming back here in around six months. I have nowhere for Flounder to go. He's a great dog. My mom won't take him. Is there any way you would consider watching him?"

"Of course I would. Let me text Grady."

She typed on her phone as I opened the present. It was a picture of Erik and me staring at each other in the pool the day he took my class. My breathing slowed as the memory took over and my body felt heavy. I was so conflicted. Hard as I tried to fight it, I still cared about him very much. And he'd been extra sweet to me lately, so it was impossible to stay mad. All through dinner last night, I had warmed up to the thought of being brutally honest with him about my insecurities about his intentions toward me and about my future plans. I had considered that maybe I had been wrong about him using me to snag a client. The conversation had focused mostly on Erik's impressive career, and I hadn't felt at all like he had been using me.

In fact, I believed now with a hundred percent certainty that he just wanted me by his side and I obviously had blown the whole thing out of proportion. Yes, he had mentioned that maybe I would be good at working at

TritonFix, but his reasoning was correct. Many Olympians were motivational speakers.

And as angry as I had been with him that night he asked me, I had no intention of using him. Even so, I wanted to try Dirty Name again.

Unfortunately, my feelings toward Erik didn't matter. He had again reiterated his opinion that women shouldn't be SEALs. And that was a deal breaker for us.

We couldn't be together…no matter how much I wanted it to work out.

Isa looked back up at me. "Grady said no problem. But wait, why didn't you ask Erik?"

Think fast. "Oh, I would've. But he deploys so much."

"That's right. Well, don't worry about Flounder. We will take great care of him."

"Thanks. You don't know how much this means to me. And thank you again for this picture. I love it."

"You're welcome."

The guests began to arrive. As I taught my final class, my thoughts returned to Erik. I had just over twenty-four hours left with him, and then I would have to say goodbye. How could I now live without him? I craved him. Who would I turn to when I needed support? Who would write him letters and tell him how much he was loved when he was deployed? The thought of disappearing from his life was ripping my heart out. Within the next two weeks, I'd be reporting for Officer Candidate School.

But in six months I would return to this island.

I would become the first female Navy SEAL. And maybe, just maybe, Erik would amend his views on women in combat. If he did, perhaps we would have a chance of then starting a real relationship. But I wouldn't hold my breath. As Erik had reminded me about his buddies' who had drowned, sometimes holding your breath was the end of your world.

25

ERIK

I woke with Aria cuddled on my chest, her long hair splayed across the pillow. A surge of lust flowed through me. It was Sunday morning, and I wanted to spend all day with her in bed. I slipped out of the covers careful not to wake her and let Flounder outside. Her dog ran around the tiny yard his ears flapping in the ocean breeze. A great dog, a gorgeous woman in bed, my idea of the perfect Sunday.

A few minutes later, Aria emerged from the bedroom rubbing her eyes.

I greeted her with a kiss. "Morning, babe."

"Morning. You hungry? I could make us some breakfast."

"I've got a better idea. Why don't we hop in my car and get

brunch in Cardiff-by-the-Sea? It's a great little beach town."

She didn't reply, just stared at me with a furrowed brow.

"Do you have any other suggestions?"

"No." She paused. "Okay, actually I do. You're going to think I'm crazy, but ever since I ran the "O" course, I'm obsessed with Dirty Name. Is there any way you will take me back to base so I can try it? Once I master it, we can head up the coast."

"Babe, it's our last day together before you leave."

"I know. And we can spend the rest of the day doing whatever you want. Can't we go for just an hour?"

What the fuck? "No. It's my day off. The last thing I want to do is go to work. I know men about to go through BUD/S who don't even practice on the weekend. Just forget about it."

She shook her head. "I can't. You don't understand . . . I just have to complete it to move on. It's this thing I have. It's going to drive me insane."

I studied her face. She made strong eye contact with me, and her posture was erect with her chest jutting out. Determined, resolute.

Part of the reason I had pursued her was for this very

reason—that she was a champion. It would be ridiculous for me to begrudge that quality now.

"It isn't built for women because the second log hits right at your breast bone. You have to catapult yourself up and land on your waist."

She nodded. "Yes, I know. I've studied videos since I failed."

Studied videos? What? Why? Was she watching Youtube clips? "It's just an obstacle course. You've won a gold medal. Who gives a fuck if you don't complete it? It's not like you're training to be the first female SEAL."

Her mouth flew open, but she quickly shut it.

And for a second a wild crazy thought crossed through my head.

Maybe she was.

Holy shit.

That could've explained why she had been so mad when I'd said that I didn't think women should be SEALs. Why she was being evasive about her training. Why she was so damn determined to finish Dirty Name.

I rubbed the back of my neck and stared at her. Not as a woman, not as a girlfriend, but as a warrior.

I objectively assessed her. She wasn't anything like the type of women who I thought would want to become SEALs. Why would she give up her career, her sport, and her endorsements to join the military?

Then again, Kyle had.

My superior officer Kyle had traded in his baller lifestyle for a life in the Teams. Kyle had done it because he believed in our mission. But he had also once confided in me, that he had also done it because he wanted a challenge.

I bet Aria felt the same way.

And her father had been a SEAL. Maybe she was doing this as a way to create some type of connection with the father she had never met?

Heat rose in my chest. Was she playing me? Using me to get an edge?

I forced my mind to calm and pushed those crazy thoughts out of my head.

No. I had it wrong. That wasn't it at all. She was just a driven champion. An Olympian. A feminist. A woman who would stop at nothing to achieve her goals. She probably saw Dirty Name as some sort of American gladiator like challenge. Hell, maybe we could team up together and win one of those couples' fitness events. And no doubt, we would win.

I exhaled and relaxed my shoulders. "Fine, champ. I'll take you to the course for one hour and work with you. But that's it. If you don't complete it, you need to just move on. And for the rest of the day, we're going to relax. No training, no workouts, no ocean swims. I want pizza and beer. Deal?"

"Deal." She hugged me. "Thank you so much, babe. This means a lot to me. I feel like you're the only person I've ever met who understands my drive."

"I do, but here's the thing. Everyone fails. When a member of my Team tells me he has failed, I say good. Not because I'm an asshole, not because I don't care, but because every time you fail you have the opportunity to improve."

Her mouth contorted. "But that's the thing, Erik. Of course, I've failed. I never told you this, but a few years before the Olympics, I fumbled a body jump at the Collegiate national championships. I cost my team the gold. I was humiliated, filled with shame. My mom never lets me hear the end of it and my coach couldn't even look me in the eye. But I regrouped and improved. I've never quit, and I'm not going to start now."

I embraced the woman in front of me as my heartbeat quickened. I wasn't just attracted to her; I respected her. She was the type of woman who wouldn't give up on anything that was important to her. The type of woman who had her own interests and goals and could be faithful to me when I was fighting a war on the other side of the globe. I'd only known her for a month, but my feelings toward her were not casual.

I was falling in love with her.

Mr. Johnson was right. I should marry her.

26

ARIA

We cruised down to the base on our bikes. I loved the feeling of the ocean breeze blowing through my hair and the scent of the salt water tickling my nostrils. This life was the life I wanted to live. Eric supported me, unlike any person I have ever met. If he could only accept my career path, I knew we could make it work. Maybe if I mastered Dirty Name today, it would give me the strength to tell him. And he would see that I could pass BUD/S.

My mom had always pushed me, but it was for her benefit not for mine. She used my success to validate herself. As if raising an Olympian somehow proved that she was a good mother.

News flash it didn't.

My mom had sacrificed for me, no doubt, but she was cruel and emotionally abusive. I frequently felt that my only worth to her was what I could accomplish and that she didn't love me for me.

Erik, on the other hand, pushed my boundaries. Ever since I'd met him only a month ago, he had already had a positive effect on my happiness.

As icing on the cake, unbeknownst to him, he was also giving me an advantage to help me achieve my goal.

And after our dinner the other night, I was even more impressed by him. I wanted him to succeed. I was proud to be by his side. I could help him as much as he could help me.

I think I'm in love with him.

Once we arrived on base Erik led me to the "O" course. This time I was in luck as a bunch of BUD/S instructors were training candidates nearby. Around twenty men stood on the shore of the beach holding Swift boats above their heads. These were the men who had completed hell week last week. The winners. The sight of my future filled my soul with adrenaline. I was so close to my dream that I could taste salt water in my mouth and feel the sand embedded in my skin.

Erik turned to me. "Okay, champ, we're going to try this again. Place both of your feet hip distance apart, and jump so your hips wrap around the first hurdle."

I took a deep breath and focused on the hurdle. For years, I'd worked with a sports psychiatrist, and I had learned to practice creative visualization. How to psych myself out before competitions. Imagine my body executing the flawless routine had become my daily mental practice.

Dirty Name would be no match for me.

I steadied my feet on the log, bent in a squat position, and jumped on the hurdle.

Smack. My body hit with a thud and dropped into the sand.

"Again." Erik's voice was calm and reassuring. Just what I needed.

I jumped again, with the same disastrous result.

And again.

And again.

For the next fucking hour, I jumped so many times that my entire body ached. I should've given up, but I couldn't stop. Like an addict, I kept returning to the starting point, unwilling to accept defeat.

I jumped again, this time face planting against the wood, splitting my lip open. I wiped the blood off my mouth, picked myself off the dirt, and walked back to the starting point.

Erik ran over to me. "Okay, babe, that's enough. Seriously. You did a great job, and I'm proud of you. But you need to give it up. I'm going to call it."

"No." My voice shook. "You have to let me try again. I can do it. I've almost got it."

He pulled me into him and held me tight. "Hey, what's with you? Why is this so important to you? You act like it's life and death. It's not like you're one of those guys out there whose career depends on this course." He pointed to the BUD/s candidates, now riding the waves in their boats.

Ha. He would reexamine every bit of our relationship in his head next year when he learned the truth.

But right now, I couldn't deal with him. Like a petulant child, I stormed off.

He caught up to me. "Aria, what the fuck is going on with you? You are blowing hot and cold with me. I get it. You're competitive. But you can't win every time. And it's okay."

I turned to him, my face red and blotchy, the metallic taste of blood dripping down my throat. I couldn't hold back any longer. My emotions burst onto the sand. "It's not okay. You have everything. You're gorgeous, have a dream career, and a family who loves you. All I have is winning. I have no close friends, I never met my father and I never will, and my mom is abusive and uses me. I have nothing.

No one cares about synchro. Winning is the only thing I've ever been good at."

God, I sounded pathetic, but I couldn't hold back.

He clutched my shoulders and forced me to look at him. "You have me. I fucking love you. I can't fight it anymore. Don't you get that? I love you, Aria, though I'm not sure why, because honestly, you're a fucking mess, but I love you anyway. I've never met a woman like you. You're everything I've ever wanted. I can make you happy. We could be the best team. We'd be unstoppable together."

OMG! Did he just say he loved me? My heart leaped for joy. I was in love with him, and he was in love with me. We loved each other. He had seen my quirkiness, my madness, and yet still loved me.

But I couldn't tell him how much I loved him.

No. No.

There was no room in my world for love. None. Not now. Definitely not now.

And he may love me now, but his love would turn to hate when he realized the secret I had been keeping from him.

He would leave me the second he found out I had joined the Navy on a BUD/S contract.

My hands shook and my vision blurred. How had I let this

get so far? This was supposed to be a summer fling and nothing more.

I had to end this.

I had to end this *now*.

I stared at this fine ass man in front of me. A man who I never thought in my wildest dreams would be attracted to me, let alone tell me he loved me. I prayed for the strength to tell the only guy I had ever loved goodbye.

"Love me? You don't even know me. You don't know anything about the real me."

He shook his head and clasped my hands in his. "You're wrong, sweetheart. I do know you. I see you, Aria. The real you. You are so determined and strong. You will stop at nothing to win. You are worthy of being loved. Please, stop shutting me out. Let me love you."

I choked down my sobs, refusing to let him see me cry. Let him see on my face how much I cared about him.

How much I loved him, too.

But unfortunately for both of us, I didn't love myself.

"You really want to know who I am? I'm a liar. I'm a fraud. I use people. If you knew who I really was, you would want nothing to do with me. Goodbye Erik."

And I stormed off the base back to the Hotel Del, leaving my pretty sea foam cruiser, and my man, behind.

My body was battered and bruised. But at least it was in one piece.

Unlike my heart.

27

ERIK

I stood there in the sand as Aria stomped off, sand from her boots flying in my face. What the fuck had just happened?

Had she literally just dumped me because I wouldn't let her keep trying Dirty Name? What the hell was wrong with her? Why was that goddamn obstacle so important to her? More important to her than I was?

And she had just told me she was a liar. What had she been talking about? How had she lied to me?

Dammit. Why had I let my guard down around her? I had even considered a future with her. This was my fucking fault. Not hers. She had told me from day one she didn't want anything serious because she wasn't going to be in town, but my dumb ass pursued her anyway. As a SEAL, I tried to push away from my emotions, focus on the facts.

But the fact was my heart had just detonated into a thousand pieces.

I grabbed her stupid bike and mine and walking both bikes back to my garage.

What the fuck was I going to do with this bike? I could've given it to Holly, but she already had a bike. I could donate it somewhere or give it to one of my buddy's wives.

But maybe, one day, Aria would return. Apologize for flipping out on me.

Until I heard from her again, I would keep the bike, and try not to remember how happy she looked riding it.

28

ARIA

SIX MONTHS LATER

O n a cold winter day, my plane touched down in San Diego. Had it really been six months since I'd left my heart here? I was so ashamed of running out like a child. And now I was back. Would I run into Erik? I wondered if he was even stateside or if he was deployed? As much as I missed him, I secretly hoped he was deployed so I wouldn't run into him. Until after I had passed BUD/S. I didn't need that distraction. One look at him on base and I would lose all my focus.

Even worse than my fear of confronting him was how much I missed him. I had deluded myself into thinking I would be able to get over him so easily. But unfortunately, that wasn't the case. I dreamt of him every night, and he filled my thoughts every second of the day. Every time I achieved a goal in my pre-BUD/S training, he was the first person I wanted to call. I had even stalked him on Facebook. Each time I refreshed his page, my heart stood still for a second, because I dreaded seeing a profile picture of him with his arm wrapped around a girl. But luckily for me, his picture remained only of him. Either way, I knew my obsession with him wasn't healthy. I hoped that one day after I completed BUD/S, I could see him and get some closure. And better yet, I dreamed that he would give me another shot.

Isa and I remained in constant contact regarding Flounder. I hadn't told her either that I had joined the Navy. Once I made it through hell week, I planned to apply to live off base and rent a place in Coronado for Flounder and me.

I waited at the baggage claim for my luggage and then boarded the bus for the Naval Special Warfare base. As we drove over the Coronado bridge, my mind flashed back to my first kiss with Erik. Gah, what was wrong with me? I had to push him out of my mind now, or there was no chance of me succeeding.

At least Officer Candidate School had been easy. Twelve weeks seemed like a breeze compared to what I was in for at BUD/S.

There was only one thing I dreaded more than seeing Erik.

Dirty Name.

I had studied so many videos since I'd left San Diego. And

though it looked so easy on tape, it was a mental block for me now.

Like riding a bike had been.

Until Erik.

He had been the one to force me to overcome my biking fear.

I needed him to help me conquer my biggest fear of all. Dirty Name.

But I'd blown any opportunity of that happening.

At this point, it was psychological. It had to be.

As we passed the Del, my heart hitched. Seeing the pool where I had met Erik, passing his condo, gazing at the ocean where we had made love, it was too much for me. I had to stop thinking about him.

The bus pulled into the gate, and my heart pounded in my chest as I scanned the men for any sign of Erik. But luckily there wasn't any. Blowing out a relieved breath, I focused on what was ahead of me. Tomorrow I would start with Physical Training Rehabilitation and Remediation for a few weeks before I joined the Indoctrination Phase.

Then I would start First Phase. The first woman in history to be in BUD/S.

I couldn't wait. Bring it.

One more step toward my goal. My destiny. My future.

If I failed, then I would have given up my love for nothing.

But if I succeeded, then maybe it would be worth it. Maybe Erik would even understand that I had had no choice but to break up with him. I would be able to prove to him that a woman could pass BUD/S and he would finally realize how wrong he had been.

He would forgive me for deceiving him, and I would forgive him for his antiquated views.

Any maybe he would love me again.

29

ARIA

Today was the first day of BUD/S.

I had been surprised when I had found out that I wasn't the only female in the pipeline.

But it didn't matter. I was the only one who remained.

One hundred twelve men and three women entered the pre-training program five weeks ago.

Eighty men and one woman remained.

I was officially the first female to ever join BUD/S.

Hooyah! Let's do this.

I glanced around the outside near the barracks. The concrete was damp from the early morning dew, but I knew soon enough it would be drenched in sweat and water, sprayed from hoses of our instructors.

Travis, a tall, skinny eighteen-year-old boy from Minnesota, stood next to me, both of us shivering in the cold pre-dawn air. "You ready? Someone always drops night one."

I looked at him dead on and punched his arm. I knew the key to succeeding was being treated like one of the guys. "Absolutely. Bring it."

"Awesome. Let's warm up." He dropped to the ground and attempted some flutter kicks.

Before I dropped down also, I studied his form. "Hey, I noticed you rest your legs on the ground between sets."

He nodded. "Yeah. I want to take a break every chance I get. They will destroy us."

"No, don't do that. I'm a swimmer. You need those hip flexors strong, so we can pass our ocean swim test. Let me show you a good stretch." I knelt next to him and showed him how to stretch deep, putting him in the correct position. He returned the favor by placing pressure on my back and helping me deepen my own stretch.

"Thanks, *Demi*. I hope you make it. I'm rooting for you."

Demi. My newly anointed nickname. G.I. Jane in the flesh. I smiled, touched by his support. Just like in synchro, I knew I was only as strong as my partner. "Hey, let's make a pact. Let's promise each other we won't quit. We can be swim buddies."

He hesitated. Maybe he didn't want to be paired with a woman.

"I'd be honored. Hooyah."

"Hooyah."

I was pumped. I couldn't wait. Nothing could stop me now.

We stood in line, next to the other men. Six SEALs in dark blue instructor shirts ran out. I scanned their faces, preparing myself to meet for the first time the men who would train us.

But as the first instructor stood in front of the group, I gasped.

A man stood front a center. His dark bangs, skimming his deep blue bedroom eyes. His tanned, tattooed arms flexing under his shirt. His perfectly chiseled face and strong jaw sneering at me.

Oh fuck. Oh no.

It was Erik.

My heart dropped, and my legs quivered.

His eyes met mine, and I forced myself to keep my gaze steady as my bottom lip quivered. A sudden coldness hit my core, and it wasn't from the chilly winter night. I blinked back tears. I refused to cry. The first female BUD/S candidate couldn't cry under any circumstances.

It couldn't be him. This couldn't be happening to me. What was this cruel twist of fate? All the ways I'd dreamed of us meeting again, this had never been in the realm of possibilities.

All my hard work would be for nothing.

For the first time since I'd set out to become a SEAL, I doubted that I would succeed. And it wasn't because of my physicality. It was a mental game. Erik knew me better than anyone. I had confessed to him my insecurities and confided in him about my father. He knew me.

And he could break me.

My mind failed to comprehend what he was yelling about, unable to grasp the depth of my nightmare.

For Erik—my ex, the man I'd lied to and left, the only guy I'd ever loved was my instructor.

And I was his student.

30

ERIK

The second my shift was over, I bolted out of the compound. Fuck my fucking life. Aria was the first female in BUD/S. I couldn't believe it even though I had seen her with my own eyes.

I hadn't been blind. I had suspected her plan once but then dismissed it as me being paranoid.

I walked into my office and slammed the door behind me.

But no sooner than I had sat down, Kyle appeared at my door. He knocked, and I signaled for him to come in.

"Commander Anderson, I'd like a word." His face was stern, his brow furrowed.

Oh fuck. "Sure, sir."

Kyle sat in front of me. "By now you know about Aria. I

wanted to warn you sooner, but I was forbidden by the Admiral to tell you. He wants her to succeed. He didn't want to risk you getting upset and approaching her during Indoc and convincing her to quit."

The Admiral knew? This was even worse than I imagined. "I understand. I swear I had no idea she planned to be a SEAL."

He nodded. "I believe you. But the problem is, the media doesn't."

The media? What the fuck was he talking about? "I'm sorry, sir. I don't understand what you are talking about."

He grabbed his phone and handed it to me. "Here."

My eyes focused on the screen. An article from Daily Mail. I read the headline, and my heart sank.

"EXCLUSIVE: This is the hunky Navy SEAL boyfriend of Olympic Gold Medalist Aria Clements—who inspired her to become the first female Navy SEAL."

What the fuck? There was a fucking picture of me staring at her in the pool at the Del, wearing that ridiculous sparkly pink tail.

I forced myself to read on. My stomach was completely nauseated as I realized my career was over.

- Aria Clements, 23, had been dating military officer 25-year-old Erik Anderson last summer.
- The couple met in Coronado where he is based at the Naval Amphibious Base.
- Aria, a graduate of Stanford University, won the Olympic Gold medal in synchronized swimming at the last summer games.
- A top graduate of the U.S. Naval Academy in Annapolis, MD, Erik was described in his yearbook as "known for his love of fast cars and faster women."

My blood boiled and every muscle in my entire body tensed. My name, my picture was splashed over the internet. I swiped back on his phone to the news feed, and my fears were realized. It was the number one story on the site.

Fuck. My. Life.

I slammed my fist into the desk.

Kyle stood up and placed a hand on my shoulder. "It's okay, man. This will die down. My name and face were on the cover of People when I married Sara. And I'm still here."

"I'm begging you, sir. Please put me on Second Phase and then switch me back to First Phase when she quits. I can't see her. I can't be around her."

Kyle shook his head. "I'd love to, but my hands are tied. The Admiral believes that you are the only person who can help her pass. You will remain a First Phase instructor."

God no. "Sir, no. I can't. I won't help her. She lied to me. She betrayed me."

"Look Anderson. This is work, suck it up. She's a job to you now. The thing is everyone believes she is qualified and they want to see a woman graduate. She was in the top ten of her Indoc class. I'm ordering you to help her. Not bend our standards, we will never do that. But you will help her. As her instructor. You are strictly forbidden from seeing her during your off time. I mean it. I'm sorry. This will all blow over once she graduates."

"If she graduates."

He glared at me. "She will graduate. Be sure of it. In fact, make sure of it. Good night."

Kyle walked out of the room, and I grabbed my own phone. It was lit up with hundreds of texts and missed calls. My email box was also flooded.

Fuck. I'd be the laughing stock of the SEAL team.

I found the flask of whiskey in my drawer and knocked back a drink. But even the liquor did little to calm my nerves.

I would be her instructor, but I would teach her the same as any other candidate. I would not help her outside of class. She would get no special treatment.

Since she'd vanished from my life, I'd missed her. Every day of my last deployment I fantasized about fucking her again, even just spending the day with her.

But no more.

Yes, I had loved her.

But I despised her now. That bitch had used me. And the only thing I was certain of at this moment was that I would never love her again.

31

ARIA

The instructors ran us ragged for eight hours straight, changing shifts halfway through. Four men had rung the bell before the night was over. Once realization set in that the instructors weren't going to let up, that this torture was only the beginning, the men who were not committed bailed.

But I remained.

We were finally dismissed to our barracks rooms. I had been lucky enough to live alone since I was the only woman left. The rest of the men went to the chow hall and hit the showers.

But I had to find Erik.

BUD/S candidates were allowed to leave the base. Some of

the married ones even lived in town with their wives and kids.

I flashed my ID and walked off base. Seven months ago, I had only been allowed on base with Erik. Now, I had my own ID card.

Though my calves burned, I ran across the beach. Straight to Erik's condo.

I pressed the elevator and exited on his floor, remembering the first night he brought me here after we had made love in the ocean.

I stood in front of his door, working up the urge to knock. I finally rang the doorbell. After a few agonizing seconds, the door flew open.

Erik stood there, his hair wet, his shirt off, in nothing but a towel.

His body looked even more ripped than I had remembered. How was that even possible? His skin was tanner; his muscles were bigger; his abs were more defined.

Fuck, was he trying to torture me?

His fresh woodsy scent drove me wild, and I couldn't help but stare at his happy trail that led to his beautiful cock. I wanted to pounce on him like a feral cat, suck him off, make him need me, show him how much I loved him.

His eyes scanned the hallway, then without a word, he grasped my arm and pulled me inside.

"What the fuck are you doing here, Aria? You can't come to my place. I'm your fucking instructor. You got that? Get the fuck out of here."

"No, please." I pleaded. "Just give me five minutes."

"Five minutes? No. You don't get to talk, woman. I'm in control. I'm in charge. You fucking used me, dammit. You used me to get an edge in training. How dare you show up here tonight. Who the hell do you think you are? You ruined my fucking life. I wish I never met you."

His words hurt worse than the four hundred pushups he had inflicted on me earlier.

"How did I ruin your life?"

He grabbed his phone and thrust it into my hand. "This. Have you seen this?"

One look at the screen and guilt consumed me. There was a picture of Erik and me in the pool at the Del staring at each other. There was another picture of us dressed as Wonder Woman and Aquaman at Isa's party. And a final picture of us on the "O" course, with him helping me with Dirty Name.

"Oh my god. No, Erik. I had no idea. None. You have to

believe me! Who took these pictures? Who sold them? I know it wasn't Isa, she would never—"

A vein popped on his neck. "I don't give a fuck who took the pictures. They are out there. You have ruined my career."

"I'm so sorry, Erik. I never wanted to hurt you. I tried to tell you, but I was scared about how you would react."

He pointed his finger at me. "Did you ever think that when this got out, you would ruin my career? No, you didn't. You are too self-absorbed to think of anyone but yourself."

A lump grew in my throat. "That's not fair. There is no way I could predict this happening."

"'I don't care if you are the first woman in BUD/S. You will fail. I'll make fucking sure of it. You will ring that fucking bell. Not because you're not strong enough, not because you lack endurance, but because you're a liar. You're deceptive. You have no integrity. You don't have what it takes to be a SEAL. Now get the fuck out of here."

I dropped to my knees. "Please. I'm begging you. Just please listen to me. I love you."

His eyes shot daggers at me. "*Love me?* You love me? You don't have a fucking clue what love is. I would've done anything for you. Anything. Do you know that? I was crazy about you. I saw a future with us. But you used me. You ghosted me. And now you show up here and make me the laughing stock of the Teams. You make me sick. I can never be with you. Never."

I placed my hand on his waist, but he pushed it off. "I'm sorry. I didn't have a choice. You told me you didn't think women should be SEALs. You wouldn't have supported me. I didn't want to date you. In fact, I told you no when you asked me out because I didn't want any complications. But you asked me out in front of your family. And you wore me down, so I figured why not? What could it hurt?"

"Gee thanks," he snarled.

I withered under his icy glare but forced myself to go on. "I didn't want to fall for you. I fought it every step of the way. But I couldn't help it." I sniffled, and a tear rolled down my cheek. "I fell in love with you, Erik. I *still* love you—nothing has changed for me. Time has stood still for my heart. When I realized that I loved you, I knew I should've told you about joining, but I couldn't. I was scared to death. I've never been so scared of anything in my life. You have to believe me."

For a second, I thought I had gained an ounce of understanding. He pursed his lips and focused on my face.

"I don't believe you. I don't want anything to do with you. You are my student. And you won't be for long. You will ring that goddam bell, no matter what the brass tells me. The sooner, the better. Goodbye, Aria."

He grabbed my wrist, pushed me out of his place, and slammed the door.

I couldn't move. The emotion I'd been holding in for months poured out. The sobs came heavy, my chest contracting.

He had been right. I should've been honest. But I had been so scared because of his strong feelings about women in combat. Couldn't he realize that? How could I have ever told him the truth?

I pulled myself together and left the building.

Erik was right about my deception.

But he was wrong about one thing.

I would never ring that bell.

32

ERIK

T he next morning, I had the balls to dawn shift. Today I would make sure she dropped. Kyle had given me an out. He had told me that we wouldn't lower our standards. Well, she wouldn't be able to meet them.

I was still so fucking pissed she had never told me she had joined the Navy. But she had been right about one thing.

I would've broken up with her if I had known she had wanted to be a SEAL.

How had I missed the signs? They were all there. Her excitement when I let her on base. Her anger when I told her that I didn't think women should be in combat. Her obsession with Dirty Name.

Dirty Name.

Yes! That was it. Dirty Name was her Achilles Heel. She

had spent an hour trying to conquer it but had been unable to. It had been a mental block for her.

It would be the reason she would fail.

My skin tingled with excitement. Because I knew she already had the run times and she had a great time in the ocean swim.

And she would never quit.

But if you don't pass the "O" course in BUD/S, you fail.

And she would fail.

I laced up my boots and ran down to the base. Devin caught up with me.

"Nice tail, man. Though I think lavender is more your color."

"Fuck off."

"At least we don't have to take bets about which one of us will bang her first. You already hit that."

I smacked him. "Shut your fucking cock holster. Don't you talk about her like that. Got it, rock star?"

Devin smirked. "Relax, man. I thought you hated her. I'll be happy to take her off your hands." He knelt on the ground and clasped his hands together. "Yes, Instructor Xander. Please let me suck your cock.'"

Rage pulsated through my body, and I slammed him against a locker. "What the fuck did I just tell you? If I hear you or any other guy harassing her, I'll fuck you up. Am I clear?"

I released him, and he straightened his shirt. "Whatever, bro. I'm just fucking with you. I knew you still wanted her."

"Fuck you."

I stormed away from him, trying to put my mind on straight. Of course, I still wanted to fuck her. She was gorgeous, and I'd never forget for the rest of my life how warm her pussy felt in that cold ocean. How I fucked her raw against the wall. How she had been my dirty girl.

But it didn't matter anymore. I could never be with her again.

I walked down to the beach to join the other instructors on the earlier shift.

The recruits were linked arm and arm in the surf as the waves crashed over them. The men had their shirts off, and Aria was wearing a sports bra. Some of the men were gasping for breath; others were gagging on the salt water.

But not Aria. She lay in the middle of the shore, her bra sandy and wet, and took deep breaths when each wave passed over her.

She didn't seem stressed. She didn't seem frustrated. It was almost as if she was calm. Completely centered and zoned. What the fuck? This wasn't yoga—this was surf torture.

I grabbed the microphone. "Get wet and sandy."

The class ran up the beach, dropped and rolled in the sand.

She ran in front of me, her body covered in sand head to toe. Some of the other men hadn't followed my orders—leaving portions of their body clean. But not Aria.

I ignored her and yelled at another man. "Hey, I see your chest and arms aren't covered. I told you to get sandy. When I give you an order, you follow it. Is that clear?"

"Hooyah, Instructor Anderson."

"Now get sandy."

I stepped away from the group and strode over to Kyle. "How'd she do on the run?"

He smirked at me. "Thirty-one minutes. She was one of only ten who passed. Not the fastest time but she made it. And she was second in the ocean swim. I'll be honest with you; I think she's going to make it."

I looked back over at her, doing mountain climbers in the sand. Her body was in plank position as her knees alternated stepping under her chest.

Some of the men's hips were raised in the air, but not Aria's. She maintained her flat back and alignment.

Kyle was right—she could make it. The only thing that stood in the way of her and that trident was Dirty Name.

And me.

33

ARIA

E rik hadn't even acknowledged my existence today, which I guess was a good thing. I refused to think about what he had said to me the other night.

I only had one thing on my mind.

Dirty Name.

Erik stood in front of us. "Today you will attempt the obstacle course. For most of you, this will be the first time you've ever tried it." He shot me a dirty glare, and I shot it right back to him. "Many of you will fail. If you do, we will drop you. You must complete this course in less than fifteen minutes. Let me show you how it's done."

And there Erik went, sprinting through the course like it was a hopscotch on a child's playground. Fuck that guy.

This time he used a different technique on Dirty Name.

Instead of using his wrists to pull himself up, he took a running jump off the log and then landed with both feet planted firmly on the first hurdle. Damn show off. What was he? A ninja?

He finished the course and walked over to the group, a cocky smirk on his face.

Why did he have to be so hot?

I centered my mind, focused on my breath. I could do this. I would complete Dirty Name. Today.

My classmates ran in front of me, but I quickly over took them. My agility came in handy up the ropes.

And I had the advantage of having run this before.

But then, it stood in front of me. Dirty Name. The obstacle that had been the death of my relationship with Erik.

I would not allow it to be the death of my dream.

Just as I was about to jump, Erik ran beside me.

"Clements. Are you going to fall again? You're a goddamn officer, an Olympian."

"No, Instructor."

Like a cat, I crouched on the log as I had done so many times in my mind and sprung up, leaping to the hurdle. My arms reached it this time, and I grasped them around it, hugging it for dear life, but I lost my grip and fell to the ground.

Fuck.

"That was pathetic, Clements. What is wrong with you? How hard is it to do one leap? Is this like the time you fucked up that body leap at nationals and caused your team to lose the championship? Just like you will cause good men to lose their lives due to your incompetence? That didn't even remotely resemble perfection. And it's because you are inside your tiny little brain defeating yourself. Do it again!"

Fucking asshole. I hated him. How dare he bring up something I told him in confidence out here. He was trying to shake me, but I wouldn't let him.

I ran back to the log, praying this time would be the one. I was so close. I squatted low and propelled myself up to the hurdle, my palms slamming against the wood.

"You failed, Aria. This isn't the Olympics. There is no prize for 2nd place. We call it first place loser. You're a loser. If you don't master this hurdle, you will be dropped. Is that understood?"

"Yes, Instructor Anderson."

"Drop down and give me one hundred pushups. If you

mess up, start again. If your chest isn't parallel with the floor, your ass better be up in the air. Is that clear?"

"Yes, Instructor Anderson."

I dropped to the sand and knocked out my pushups, making sure to eat the sand with every damn one.

Over the past week, I'd become a connoisseur of sand. Though I preferred the salty aftertaste of the sand closer to the shore, the sand on the "O" course at least wasn't mixed with tire tracks residue like the sand that was alongside our running path.

I would not give up. I would conquer Dirty Name. I would spend every free second I had practicing it until I made it.

I looked up and caught Erik staring at me. But his normally angry scowl toward me was absent. He seemed to be eye fucking me. And was that a smile on his face?

But he had just berated me.

Hmm. Berating me was his job. . .

A thought crossed my head. I needed to see Erik again. Alone. By now he must've had time to think. He was a rational man. Maybe I could get him to really understand me. I needed him to forgive me.

It was completely risky. If we were caught together, I

would inflict even more damage on his career, and I would probably be forced out.

For the first time, I realized I wanted something even more than becoming a SEAL.

Erik.

I needed to at least let him know that what I felt for him was real. How much I still thought we would be unstoppable together. How much I craved him and wanted to make him happy. I wanted to thank him for how he had treated me when we were dating. How his belief in me made me more certain than ever that I would succeed here.

34

ERIK

Today the candidates had a timed one-mile bay swim without a wetsuit. The water was around fifty degrees. It would be a brutal one.

The candidates paired up with their swim buddies, and we tossed them off the boat into the bay.

I grabbed my megaphone. "Remember, it's mind over matter. If you don't mind, it won't matter."

Twenty minutes into the swim, I noticed that Aria's swim buddy was struggling. Usually, around this time in training, many SEAL candidates would still preserve themselves, not willing to risk failing their evolution to help their partner.

But Aria remained by his side, urging him along. Another

pair quit and came crying to the side of the boat like babies. Meanwhile, Aria and her partner arrived at the boat first out of all pairs, completing their swim in less than thirty minutes.

She was shivering when I pulled her into the boat. I sat her on the deck and handed her a towel. "Hey, you did a good job out there. I liked the way you took care of your swim buddy."

Her face brightened, but she didn't respond. Her teeth were chattering, and her skin had a bluish tint. I checked her temperature, made sure she was fine, and then focused on the pairs in the water.

And for the first time since she'd been in BUD/S, my heart softened toward her. Had I forgiven her? Could I possibly see things from her point of view? Because as hard as it was to admit, deep down I knew she had been right. If she had told me she had wanted to be a SEAL, I would've shut her down.

There was no way I would've accepted it unless I had been forced to.

Later that night, I relaxed in my office at BUD/S. I was on night duty, and most of my fellow Instructors had gone home. The quietness of the base was a welcome change of pace from the cacophony of training.

I took a moment to examine the facts.

She was top of her class. She had sailed through surf warfare.

What if she actually passed?

My phone rang. It was my sister.

"Hey. What's up, sis?"

"Oh my god, Erik. Guess what? I just got in early action to Stanford! I'm going to be able to compete on the synchro squad."

"Congrats, Holly. I'm so proud of you. Dad would be too."

"Thanks. I can't believe it. I never thought I'd get it. But Aria called her coach—"

Wait, what? "You still talk to her?"

"No. I didn't want to be disloyal to you. But the Stanford coach called me today and said that Aria had recommended me. I can't believe she did that for me, well because, well you know."

Yeah, I knew all too well. I didn't have to tell my family that Aria was back in town. Thanks to the media, everyone in the fucking world knew about my love life.

I said goodbye to Holly, grabbed a flask from my desk, and took a swig. Then I heard my door creak open.

Aria stood in front of me. Her hair was wild, and she had bruises all over her body.

"Aria—"

She placed her finger over her lips, and quietly shut the door.

"You can't be here."

She didn't respond, and before I could say another word, she ran behind me and crouched under my desk.

"Please. Will you just listen to me?"

If someone caught me with her, it would be both our asses. She'd be kicked out, and I would be disciplined.

I pushed my chair out and whispered to her, keeping my eyes staring straight ahead.

"There's nothing to left to say. I understand why you didn't tell me. I forgive you. But it doesn't matter. Our relationship is in the past. We can never be together. I need you to understand that and stop pushing me."

"I do. I get it. I'll stop. But… I miss you. So much."

I glanced down at her. "Yeah?"

Her lower lip quivered. "You don't know how many times I've thought about us. What I felt, what I *still* feel, is real." Her hand grabbed at my belt.

Fuck. This was hot and forbidden. She was under my desk. No one could see us.

"I've missed you, too." I reached down and stroked her hair. "And you're doing a good job out there."

She spread my legs open and released my cock from my cammies. "Really, Instructor Anderson? Tell me how good I am?"

"So good, baby."

She hummed and wrapped her greedy little mouth around my cock, taking me deep.

I grabbed the back of her neck, guiding her rhythm. If someone passed by the room, it would look like I was just relaxing in my chair.

"You naughty girl. I love your hot mouth. Every night in Iraq, I dreamed of you sucking me off. Show me how much you like it, Demi."

Her tongue licked around my head, and she started to roll her hand up and down my length. The combination of her mouth and her firm grip of her hand caused the pleasure to pulsate through me.

"I want to throw you over this table and fuck you from behind. Would you like that, dirty girl?"

She nodded yes. Sucking, rubbing, and licking me until I

exploded into her mouth. She licked me dry and then she placed my cock back in my pants.

"Aria, that was hot as hell. But that can't happen again. Look, I don't hate you. But you weren't honest with me. That's a huge deal breaker. And now, we're fraternizing. This will never work."

"I know. I just want you to know, no, I *need* you to know, that I loved you. I wasn't using you to pass BUD/S. No one has ever believed in me the way you did, and I'm eternally grateful for spending that month with you." Tears shimmered in her gorgeous green eyes, and the sight just about broke me. "You completely changed me. You're everything I want in a man. I need you to know how sorry I am. For not telling you my plans, for leaving you, for any damage that article caused to your career. I'm just so damn sorry."

I looked down at this beautiful, insanely brave woman under my desk. Did I still love her? Fuck. Why did this have to be so complicated?

She wiped her mouth and slipped out from under my desk, immediately facing me at attention.

"Good night."

"Good night, sir."

She turned to leave my office.

"Hey, one more thing. I'm proud of you."

She smiled and walked out the door.

One thing was clear to me. I had never met a woman as exceptional as Aria Clements.

35

ARIA

A few days later, I still hungered to taste Erik's cum on my lips again. I was high on his salty taste and masculine scent. Had he really forgiven me? Maybe we still had a chance?

It didn't matter now. I had to focus.

While the rest of my classmates enjoyed the precious few hours we were allowed to slumber, I met my enemy on the battlefield.

I had a date with Dirty Name.

I returned to the "O" course, taking a moment to marvel at the deep blue night ocean. I had two more days to conquer my fear.

For the next two hours, I ran the course, each time failing Dirty Name. I tried every technique I could think of. I went faster, I went slower, I hoisted my legs over it, under it, threw my body on top of the log, under the log, but I still couldn't complete it.

But I couldn't give up.

I looked up at the condos where Erik lived. There was a light on in his place, and I could swear he was watching me.

I needed him. Not as my lover. But as the only person who'd ever really believed in me.

With his help and support, I could pass. Without lowering the SEALs strict standards.

A lump rose in my throat. But I didn't have him anymore. I had to rely on myself.

36

ERIK

W e were two weeks into First Phase, and only forty-one members of the class remained.

One of them was Aria.

But she wasn't in the clear yet. Hell week was two days away.

And she still hadn't been able to complete the "O" course.

Every day I trained her with her classmates.

And every night, I watched her from my bedroom window, trying to jump on Dirty Name.

It was a bit past midnight. The class had to be up at four in the morning. But as I gazed out my window, I saw a small figure under the fluorescent lights, attempting to overcome her hurdle.

At this point, it was mental. She was the most exceptional performer in our class by far.

I knocked back a whiskey. One of the reasons I'd been so against women in BUD/S was I thought we would have to lower our standards.

But Aria had shown me that was far from the case. She hadn't just met our standards; she had exceeded them.

The goal of BUD/S wasn't just to haze these men. It was to ensure that they could succeed at war.

Deep down, we wanted all the candidates to succeed.

So why was I being such an asshole to Aria?

Was it because she hurt me? Humiliated me?

Or was it because I didn't think she belonged here?

Kyle had ordered me to help her. The Admiral wanted her to succeed.

If I was truly the only person who could help her pass this hurdle, why was I holding her back? If it were any other candidate, I'd help.

I hurriedly dressed and put my boots back on. I ran back to base, flashed my ID, and made my way to the "O" course.

Aria was squatting on the first log of Dirty Name. She was

filthy and battered, but I still thought she was the most beautiful woman I'd ever seen.

She turned as I walked up to her. "Please, I know I'm not supposed to be practicing. Don't kick me off the course. This is my last chance. I'm so close, I—"

I put my hand over her mouth. "I'm not here to make you stop. We're going to do this together. It's just like the bike, champ. You got this."

"Champ?" Her lips trembled, and she blinked rapidly. "You're helping me? You have no idea how much this means to me."

"I'm not helping you because of our past—I'm helping you because it's my job. I'm your instructor. That's all it is. Don't speak. Watch me."

I ran back and did a running start. Then I jumped off the log like I had done a thousand times before and landed on my waist over the hurdle, using my forearms to propel me.

I returned to Aria.

"I've done that. It doesn't work. I just can't get it."

I grasped her shoulders. "Yes, you can. Don't say that. I believe in you. You have completed both the ocean swim and run in time. You're an Olympian. You will do this now. We're going to do it together."

She nodded.

We ran back into the sand, and I held her hand. A jolt shot to my cock. Her touch always ignited me.

"One, two, three, go." I dropped her hand.

We ran together, but I stepped out of the way. She leaped up and pulled her body up with her forearms.

She started to struggle, but I cheered her on. "That's it, champ. You got it! Pull yourself up. Don't look down."

She wrapped her body around the bar using her legs and did it again on the higher hurdle, before jumping down.

"You did it!"

I ran toward her and scooped her up into my arms. Before I could stop myself, our lips met. I kissed her despite my vow that this was just business and she was no different than any other candidate. We were out in the open for the whole base to see. My mind wanted to stop but my lips didn't listen. I grabbed the back of her neck and ravished her mouth, claiming it for mine.

For now.

Forever.

She kissed me back furiously, her hands pressing against my chest before I found the strength to pull away.

"Erik, I can't thank you enough. I couldn't have done it without you. You don't know how much this means to me. I love you."

At that moment, I knew that I still loved her.

That I had never stopped.

And I refused to ever let her go.

"I love you, too."

Tears stained her cheeks. I hadn't seen her cry once during BUD/S until now.

I looked at her face in the moonlight, and I finally realized that she was going to make it. I was staring at the first female Navy SEAL.

And I was proud to be her man.

I lifted her chin up. "Stop it, champ. SEALs don't cry."

EPILOGUE

A year after I first met Erik at the pool in the Del, I stood amongst my classmates. Of the eighty-one people who had started BUD/S, only sixteen remained.

And I was one of them. I had done it. I was the first female BUD/S graduate.

My face was plastered on every magazine cover. Gold medal Olympian turned GI Jane. I was livid at the news coverage. The success of being an operator depended on my anonymity. But I knew that Erik and I would get through it together.

Erik was no longer my instructor. After our public kiss on the "O" course, Erik had been sent to Indoc until I was through with BUD/S. And I had been training all day, so we had agreed not to see each other until I graduated.

But unlike before, we had no doubts about our relationship. We had vowed that night I conquered Dirty Name to be together no matter what the costs.

And I graduated today.

I dressed in my crisp white Naval uniform and prepared to get my diploma.

The commander of the base, shook each of our hands, one by one.

"Congratulations Class 334. I welcome all of you to the Teams. Hooyah and well done."

I looked at the audience and saw that my mom was sitting next to Erik's mom and sister. Isa and Grady were also there. I hadn't spoken to my mom in months, and I didn't want to share my happy day with her. But today I would focus on my blessings and not my family drama.

I made my way down the line and shook all my instructors' hands. Erik was waiting for me at the end. Our relationship now had become an open secret. Even so, we didn't advertise the fact we were together.

I stood in front of Erik and offered him my hand. He took it, kissed it and knelt in front of me.

Oh my god.

"Champ, you earned your Trident today. But I've got

another piece of metal for you to wear." He reached into his pocket and grabbed a small velvet box. He popped it open, and I gasped when I saw a gorgeous diamond ring. "Will you marry me?"

"Yes, yes, yes! I love you."

"I love you, too."

And I knew that he truly loved me. He'd believed in me when no one else had. He'd helped me overcome my fears. He was a strong man who wasn't emasculated by my success.

And I finally believed that I deserved him.

He placed the ring on my finger and then lifted me up into his arms.

"Now, you'll always be part of my world."

THE END

Stay Tuned for the next book in the Heroes Ever After Series.

SKIN: A Rockstar Navy SEAL Romance

SKIN

Chapter One—Dax

I jerked back my head, flinging my blond hair off my face, the sweat dripping down my bare chest. My fingers remained glued to the strings, strumming the final riffs of our rock ballad. Ten thousand rabid fans mouthed the lyrics—the stadium glowed from the synchronized cigarette lighters, the night air pungent with drug fumes. A half naked girl surfed the crowd, minions throwing her on stage, as if they were offering a sacrifice, kneeling at the altar of their rock god—me. What an incredible night. I better fucking enjoy it—because tonight would be my last show, the last time I would make love to this guitar, the last time I would sing our songs. Tonight would be the night my chords would go silent.

But fuck it, tonight wasn't over yet. I was going to live it up. Fuck the finest woman in the audience, get completely wasted, maybe even trash a hotel room. My backstabbing band mates—guys I'd known since we were cub scouts—could go fuck themselves. I'd practiced in my parents' garage with these two-timing sons of bitches since before we reached puberty. We'd broken every barrier in the industry, brought heavy metal music back from obscurity, bridged the gap between rock star and celebrity.

I scanned the crowd, looking for my victim. Usual suspects milled in the crowd—bleached blonde bimbos, marked metal maidens, slutty sorority sisters. But for my last night as a rock star, I wanted someone innocent. Not a virgin, fuck no, I wanted some girl to ride me like a Harley. But I wanted a good girl, a girl who didn't sleep around, a girl who would never dare indulge in her rock star fantasy. A girl who would remember me forever.

What people didn't get about rockstars was that everything was handed to us. Yes men surrounded me, my every whim catered to. I wanted a challenge. For once in my life, I wanted to have to work for something.

My drummer Callan battled the bass drum, and my throat tightened. This was it. My final note. I plucked the last string, the sound soaring in my ears. A lump grew in my throat, and my eyes watered, but it wasn't from the smoke filled air. It was over. I clutched my beloved guitar, the instrument that had been my lifeline for so many years, and smashed it on the ground. Every bang, every slam, every crack filled me with rage. Chips of wood flew on the stage, strings popped, and I destroyed my prized possession. I glanced back at the audience, my heart pounding in my chest. I gave them a final wave goodbye, flicked off my traitorous bandmates, and exited stage left.

Publicists milled backstage, reporters shoved microphones in my face, and girls screamed when I walked by. Too easy. I wanted something real, a connection. Even though I would never be good for anything more than a one-night stand.

I grabbed a bottle of jack and took a swig; the smooth liquid coated my throat. I was hungry, but wasn't in the mood for the butter-poached lobster waiting in my room backstage. I figured I had a few seconds to make a break for the concessions, before the fans filed out. I dashed out the back door, and entered closest food stand.

Carnal Asada. Kick ass. What a cool fucking name. Mexican food in San Diego was always amazing. I was grateful to have my last show here, one of my favorite cities. I slid to the counter to order some tacos, when something besides food whet my appetite.

Jet-black hair that skimmed her back, huge tits that filled out her t-shirt, jeans that hugged her phat ass. Her plump lips were painted pink, but besides that she didn't seem to have a hint of makeup on. Wow—did this woman have any clue how naturally beautiful she was?

She barely looked up from the register. "What can I get for you?"

"I'll have two *carne asada* tacos and your number."

Her head straightened and her eyes met mine, her lashes rapidly blinking. "Oh my god! You're Dax, aren't you? I'm so sorry I didn't notice you there. What are you doing out here? You'll get mobbed."

People starting exploding out of the concert hall, and she was right, I had to get backstage. "It's cool. Bring me my food to my dressing room." I threw down a twenty-dollar bill and handed her a laminated back stage pass.

She brushed her hand through her hair, and rubbed the back of her neck. I winked at her and gave her my signature head nod. Before she could say a word, I disappeared backstage.

I stalked passed my singer, Trey. Motherfucker, tried to shake my hand. Fuck him. Fuck them all. Guy was a dick, always had been. Long time suffered of LSD, Lead Singer Disease. I was honest to god glad to be free of these fuckers, I just wished I could've left on my own terms.

I opened my dressing room, grateful that the bullshit statement about my departure wouldn't be released until tomorrow. Creative differences my ass. But I refused to be a sob story to the media. I had a plan. Tomorrow I would vanish, and I would make my own path. I was twenty-one, I had my whole life ahead of me.

I peeled off my leather pants and hopped into the shower. The hot water scalded my skin, and I scrubbed the concert off of my chest.

I heard a knock at the door. Great—dinner had arrived. And dessert.

"Dax, uhm it's Marisol, from Carnal Asada? I brought your food. I'll just leave it at the table."

Not so fast sweetheart. "Hey, hold up. I'll be out in a second."

I wrapped a towel around my waist, and opened the bathroom door. "Thanks, babe. Hey, what are you doing tonight?"

Her eyes scanned my body, dropping briefly to my cock but then focusing back on my face. "I have to clean up at the restaurant and then I was going to head home."

I walked over to her, careful to maintain eye contact. "No, you're not. You're coming to Vegas with me."

Her jaw dropped, wide enough for me to imagine my cock

in it. "Vegas? You're out of your mind. Don't you have groupies or something?"

I laughed. "Groupies bore the fuck out of me. My band-mates are assholes, everyone in my entourage is paid to tell me how fucking awesome I am. I want a good girl who wants to be bad. Are you game?"

Coming Fall 2017

AUTHOR'S NOTE

Thank you for reading my book.

If you liked it, would you please consider leaving a review?
TRITON

Also, check out my free book Conceit

For the latest updates, release, and giveaways, subscribe to
Alana's newsletter and get another free book, *Chronic*

For all her available books, check out Alana's *website* or
Facebook page.

Follow me on *Bookbub*.

ALSO BY ALANA ALBERTSON

Want more romance?

Love Navy SEALS?

Meet Erik! She will never be part part of my world. *TRITON*

Meet Pat! I had one chance to put on the cape and be her hero. *Invincible*

Meet Kyle! I'll never win MVP, never get a championship ring, but some heroes don't play games. *Invaluable*

Meet Grant! She wants to get wild? I will fulfill her every fantasy. *Conceit, Chronic, Crazed, Carnal, Crave, Consume, Covet*

Meet Shane! I'm America's cockiest badass. *Badass* (co-written with *Linda Barlow*)

Love Marines?

Meet Grady! With tattooed arms sculpted from carrying M-16s, this bad boy has girls begging from sea to shining sea to get a piece of his action. *Beast*

Meet Bret! He was a real man—muscles sculpted from carrying weapons, not from practicing pilates. *Love Waltzes In*

Love demons?

Who's haunting America's favorite ballet? *Snow Queen*

ACKNOWLEDGMENTS

I WOULD LIKE TO THANK my wonderful husband, Roger , for supporting my dreams, making Hello Fresh for me, and entertaining our boys while I write.

I would like to thank my editor, Kim Nadelson for guiding me through the romantic ARC of this book. I love working with you.

To Deb Nemeth for your amazing insight.

And to my fans! I love you!

ABOUT THE AUTHOR

ALANA ALBERTSON IS the former President of RWA's Contemporary Romance, Young Adult, and Chick Lit chapters. She holds a M.Ed. from Harvard and a BA in English from Stanford. A recovering professional ballroom dancer, she lives in San Diego, California, with her husband, two young sons, and five dogs. When she's not saving dogs from high kill shelters through her rescue Pugs N Roses, she can be found watching episodes of UnREAL, Homeland, or Dallas Cowboys Cheerleaders: Making the Team.

For more information:
www.authoralanaalbertson.com
alana@alanaalberton.com